AURORA ANGELS

Messengers to the Age of Armageddon

**PRAISE
PUBLISHING**

I will praise thy name for ever

AURORA ANGELS

Messengers to the Age of Armageddon

L.E. London

PRAISE PUBLISHING
Big Rapids, Michigan

AURORA ANGELS

© 2002 by L.E. London
All rights reserved

ISBN 0-9674425-6-7

Published by:
Praise Publishing
15955 15 Mile Road
Big Rapids, MI 49307

No part of this publication may be reproduced, stored in a retrieval system or transmitted in any way by any means, electronic, mechanical, photocopy, recording or otherwise, without the prior permission of the publisher, except as provided by USA copyright law.

Library of Congress Control Number: 2001-130973

Scripture quotations taken from the Douay-Rheims Bible.

Printed in the United States of America.

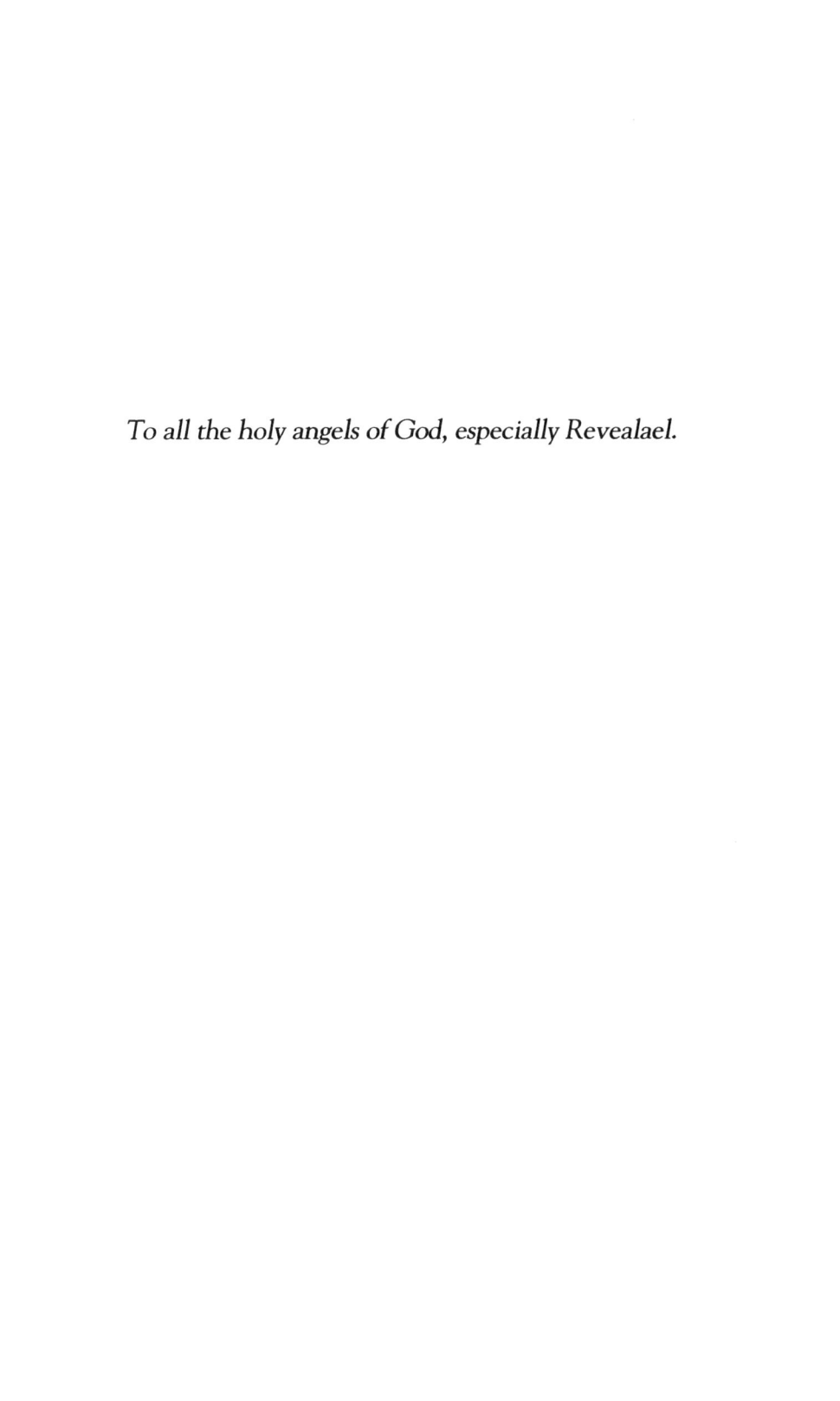

To all the holy angels of God, especially Revealael.

And he shall gather them together into a place, which in Hebrew is called Armageddon.

The Apocalypse 16:16

Prologue

Many were the days when words, like water flowing down a steady stream, flowed ever into mind. Many too the restless nights filled with strange visions of places and of beings never before seen. Through it all, illusion transformed into mystery.

The world within became a battleground, so real, where good and evil waged a war that would not end until the day that time would be no more. Still, unknown things were seen and heard, and the mind asked why these strange things should come.

A soft voice from within replied, "The time is short, and these must be revealed to a generation unaware." Confusion followed and a cry for help arose in the struggle to understand what all this was meant to be. And the voice answered, "Prophecy."

An unexpected visitor, and yet, prophecy was no stranger, as for twenty years or more its voice had called, yet, never through a story, nor in visions of such glory, nor in scenes of such evil and despair. Then, the voice said, "These must be made known."

Hesitation and doubt followed and then prayers to the Almighty, that if these words and visions were not from

Him, to be set free. But they did not leave, and their presence only grew stronger until the Spirit's anointing could not be ignored. Convincingly, the Spirit said, "Write down what has been heard and seen."

Surely, mystery follows prophecy, regardless if the message is in vision, word, or song. Whether prophecy foretells the future or forthtells of past and present, mystery with prophecy abounds. "Therefore," said the Spirit, "let the reader then pray and discern."

Now, therefore, is given the words and the visions that have been received. And understand that this you must know: Although mysteries often remain mysteries, this mystery shall be revealed to you: "The time is short and the end is near, but Armageddon, no one knew!"

CHAPTER 1

The Messenger

"No stopping now," he mumbled to himself as the wind carried his frozen breath away in a streak of white, wispy clouds, "too much at stake." Still, the bitter cold penetrated his flesh deeper with each step he forced up the hill and the sweet aroma of baked goods that had tormented his senses during this last block of his journey pleaded with him to explore its source.

Struggling to twist his head far enough to the left to compensate for the area in his left eye that had been robbed of vision by optic neuritis when he was fifteen years old, he could just barely see the small brick bakery that was hidden behind whirling clouds of snow. How he longed to linger in its delightful warmth. But no matter how hungry and cold, he would not be deterred. He had already waited far too long. Peter York was determined to reach his destination, and he refused to be late.

"Squa....awk, squa....awk, squa....awk" cried his boots against the frozen snow on the walk. Blending with the howling wind they sung a bitter melody on the weather.

"Must be the coldest day of the year," he thought, "but makes no difference. I've no time to waste."

Taking the bus from Riverton to Glory Falls made for a tight schedule, but there had been no other choice. He had no car, and surely couldn't walk fifty miles in this weather. The three-mile walk from the bus station was bad enough.

Turning his gaze forward, into the wind, he gave a sigh of relief. Though his face was again being directly pelted with freezing projectiles of icy snow, at least now, finally, he could see Saint Alphonsus Church. Solemnly upon the hill ahead of him it sat, beckoning him onward. And he picked up his pace as he thought how good it would be to enter its warmth.

Soon, he ascended the several dozen steps that rose to the entrance of the church, swung open the large oak door, and entered the shelter of the vestibule. Once inside, he brushed the snow off his heavy, tan coat and from his dark-brown walking boots and slacks with his hands. His head was another story. Snow and ice had joined with his short, black hair to form a frozen gray mat.

Using the reflection from the glass in a nearby book display, he pulled out his handkerchief and wiped down his hair and face. Until then, Peter hadn't realized the extent his flesh had been numbed by the cold. His normally light-pink facial complexion was a flaming red. His eyes, too, displayed a redness that overpowered their normally brilliant blue pupils, and his hands, ears, and nose began to tingle with pain as the warmth brought back their feeling. But at nineteen, he was young and strong. It would take much more than this small ordeal to turn him away from his mission.

Stepping into the church, he dipped his fingers into the holy water by the door and made a sign of the cross before walking up the center aisle toward the sanctuary. Though he had never before been here, this church made him feel like an old friend. With only the faint illumination that came from a light that was on in the back by the confessional and the dim glow the storm allowed through the windows, still, he could see the soaring chamber with its graceful columns, beautiful stained glass, and captivating paintings that depicted scenes from the Bible. They lifted his spirit and made him feel near the Lord.

When he reached the front pew, he slowly genuflected, entered, knelt, and humbly prayed, "Lord, have mercy on me a sinner."

Raising his head to look up toward the tabernacle, he was immediately confronted with the ultimate reality of sin and why he had come here. Above the tabernacle was the most realistic crucifix he had ever seen.

Eluding the storm and entering through a stained glass window depicting Christ carrying the lost sheep, from the chapel off to his right, a ray of sunlight illuminated the crucifix. Larger than life, the corpus mesmerized him as it hung there on its giant wooden cross. Seemingly alive, this image that appeared to bleed from the head, hands, feet, and side nearly forced one to ponder the terrible price of sin. With his head facing downward and his eyes open, it seemed like the man on the cross was looking directly at him, expecting some sort of response to the terrible agony he endured.

Peter wanted to do just that. Lately, he had thought a lot about sin and what the Lord had done. He regretted that it had taken him most of the seven years since his father's death to start thinking straight, but at least it was finally happening.

The very confusing semblance of Christianity he experienced at his and neighboring parishes over the past few years had nearly driven him completely away from Christ.

By the mercy of God, that hadn't happened. He wanted to understand the truth that Jesus had talked about. He knew the first step was to be in God's grace. He wanted to be truly alive, but to have full life he knew he needed help. He knew he needed forgiveness.

He looked at his watch. It was quarter to four. "Praise be," he thought, "still time before confession begins." Soon Father Marks would be in the confessional. He had to set his mind upon what he would say when he entered, even though he had already gone over it in his head many times. More than anything, Peter wanted to be prepared to make a good confession. He wanted to make a clean, fresh start with God.

From his heart he quietly prayed, "Thank you Lord for the opportunity you have given me this day. Please help me to make a good confession and let Father Marks be a faithful priest and say the words that you want me to hear. And Lord, I ask you to please drive the confusion from my life as you open my mind and heart to your ways. Teach me your truths and show me your ways. I realize that I can't know everything, but there are so many things that I don't understand. There are so many people that teach in your name who have confused me, Lord, and I ask that you help me to know who I should listen to. Strengthen me to serve you, for your glory. Thank you, Father, for loving me. Help me to love you more. In Jesus' name. Amen."

Abruptly, Peter was brought back to the reality around him as a soft, deep voice directly beside him echoed, "Amen!"

Startled by the voice of the unknown presence, he uncontrollably jumped back, lost his balance, and slipped off of the kneeler. While struggling to regain control and find his way back upon the kneeler in the dark church, he fought to turn his head far enough to the left to see the mysterious presence that had acknowledged his prayer. His state of surprise soon gave way to embarrassment, which quickly turned to awe.

The first thing he saw caused him to pause. It was a large foot wearing what appeared to be a golden-colored sandal. "How strange," he thought, "to wear sandals in the middle of winter."

And then, for a moment, as he looked upward and saw the white robe, he thought his visitor was an altar boy. But it was all so very unusual. The stranger's garment was made of some iridescent material Peter had never before seen. Its color changed. From white, to blue, or green, and red it went, but then at other moments it radiated in a rainbow of colors all at once. "Amazing," he thought, "and in the darkness of this church."

As Peter's eyes slowly traveled upward over this unusual intruder, he was in no way prepared for what he would see. The innocent face of a boy looked back at him from the body of a huge man. Whoever he was, Peter had never before seen anyone like him. His face was clean-shaven, like Peter's, but that's where the resemblance ended. His features were all too perfect. He appeared more like a man from an ancient Greek sculpture than a real person.

The long, curly hair on his head came almost to his shoulders, but what caught Peter's attention was its color. It was the purest white hair he had ever seen. On closer analysis, the most unique feature of this man was his eyes. They were a brilliant blue that Peter could only with great difficulty look away from once he had looked into them. They seemed to penetrate his very being.

Staring at this strange individual, Peter cautiously raised himself from the kneeler and took a sitting position next to him. Although Peter was over six-foot, two-inches tall, this man dwarfed him.

Finally, after taking a deep breath, Peter gathered all his courage and asked in a shaky voice not much louder than a whisper, "Wha...what do you want?"

Without hesitation, the intruder answered in a soft, but persuasive, voice, "Nothing but to do the will of Him who sent me."

"Who is that?"

"You prayed to the Almighty One and I am His answer for you,"

"I did," came a reply that was nearly as much a question as an answer.

"You asked God for guidance and direction in your life and He sent me to help you to see and understand."

Peter was totally dumbfounded by his answer and meekly asked, "Who are you?"

Boldly, he proclaimed, "I am a messenger of God. From the beginning He has called me Revealael because to reveal is what he has called me to."

"You...you are an angel?"

"Yes. Do you not believe in angels?"

"No, no, that's not it at all," Peter explained as he raised his arms in a gesture of confusion. "I just never expected to see one. What do you wish to reveal?"

"I am one of the seven Aurora Angels of God and I have been sent to reveal the will of God to you. Ah, yes... you are wondering why it is that I am called an Aurora Angel. I will show you, but for now simply know that I will indeed reveal that fact to you in due time. First things first.

"You are thinking, 'Why would God send an angel to me? Who am I?' My answer to you is: Do not question the judgment of the Almighty! He knows all and does all to perfection. His judgment is without error. Believe me, I have known Him since the beginning and I am at all times in awe of His infinite wisdom.

"The Almighty has known your heart from before you were created in your mother's womb. From before the first day that He created time, He has known you and loved you. Be assured that nothing is beyond His grasp or His power to accomplish. He alone is the Lord of All."

"Yes...yes, I believe that," interjected Peter, "but, what does He want?"

"He heard your plea. He did not put off answering your prayer but at once started to work within your willing heart. He began immediately to lead you away from sin and to union with His will. He has, in fact, never left you. It is only you who have in times past walked away from Him.

"Almighty God has long prepared for the day that He could send His servant to bring you this answer to your prayers. That could not happen until you became receptive to His will. For one cannot really hear and understand God while he has set himself up as God's enemy. Do you know how one becomes God's enemy?"

"To disobey him," answered Peter sheepishly.

"Yes. The strongest walls in all the universe are built of sin. But there is much more. I hear your mind. Do not be afraid. I know you cannot fully comprehend what it is that I speak of. It will be revealed gradually to you so that you may understand. I will reveal to you that which God says you need to know.

"Before I show you what you have been destined to see, understand that you should not be misled by what I can do in revealing God's will. All that I have and can do comes from God. I am simply a small reflection of His awesome glory. I have only that which He gave me. To compare my power to that of the Almighty would be like comparing one grain of sand to all those of the seashore.

"In fact, even that would not be an accurate comparison, for I have absolutely nothing that did not come to me through the Lord's great love. He is my God and I am merely His servant and messenger.

"But, I am not here to only reveal myself to you; there are things that the Lord wants you to know. These are the things you must know if you are to fulfill His plan for your life, as you have prayed to do. Much is not as it appears. You must come to understand what is truly happening around you."

"Yes, I want that," said Peter as forcefully as he could.

"Good. The time is short and there is much work to do. God desires that none perish, but He will force no one to serve Him. The Almighty has patiently worked and waited for mankind to return to Him, but soon He will wait no longer. A time is quickly coming, and in fact is already at the door, when the earth and all upon it will suddenly perish.

"But fear not. God will give the strength and wisdom necessary for victory to all that seek Him in truth and righteousness."

"What do you want me to do?" asked Peter, quite taken by all the angel had said.

"Be patient and listen carefully. I will reveal to you all that must be known about what has been, is now, and soon will be."

CHAPTER 2

The Auroras

"Please tell me more," pleaded Peter. "I want to know all that you can tell me!"

"I have much to tell you and to show you as well," assured Revealael. "There are many things that you must see if you are to understand."

"To see? Are you taking me somewhere?"

"Yes and no," the angel answered while staring upward in a thoughtful expression.

"I will be taking you to many places and you will see and feel many things, but they are not within the physical realm that you have known all your life. Though very different from the world in which you live, they are, none-the-less, just as real.

"As there is a physical reality there is also a spiritual reality, and as both are real so are both created by God and for God. The place, which I will now take you, is within the spiritual reality. You must observe what it holds.

"If you are to understand the nature of that which has happened, is now happening, and will happen in the future then you must look at all these events through the perspective of the spiritual realm. One, in fact, cannot begin to understand the meaning of the world and mankind's purpose without having at least somewhat of an understanding the spiritual realm."

Puzzled as to whether his body could enter the spiritual realm, Peter asked, "Can you do this without me dying, or are you telling me that my life is over?"

"Yes, I can take you to the spiritual realm, and no you will not die. Be not afraid. God is with you. He has sent me to be at your side to protect you and explain that which will be revealed to you. You have nothing to fear.

"I will take you into the spiritual realms of the past, the present, and the future. Through these encounters you will come to understand the great battle that is now being waged upon the inhabitants of the earth."

"You can go to the past?" blurted Peter. "Travel in time? I never thought that time travel was possible."

"For man, no," the angel carefully explained, "but for God all things are possible. In the beginning, time was created by God. It is an entity, which He controls and keeps in existence by His will; time has no power over Him. The Almighty is not limited by space or time, but rather space and time are limited by Him.

"Do not expect to be comfortable with the thought of presence without time. In your present physical state you are held fast by time's grasp and cannot see beyond it. This is the way God intended it to be for man. But for God, when His Word says that to Him a thousand years are as a day and a day as a thousand years, that is exactly the case. For to the Almighty, yesterday, today, and tomorrow are all present. Time is always at God's beckon."

"What time are we going to?"

"Many. I have much to show you. Know that what you will see, hear, and feel are true, but know also that they are not the totality of the reality. I will enable you to understand as much of the spiritual world as is possible for you while in the body. Remember, with what you experience, that the underlying truth is what is really important and not the externals.

"Are you now willing to encounter the truth?"

"Yes," answered Peter enthusiastically.

Holding out a hand, he said, "Take my hand and I will reveal it to you."

Peter took the angel's hand and immediately felt a strange warmth radiate into his hand, slowly up his arm and then throughout his body. The touch of the angel had a calming effect upon him, and he was not afraid. Suddenly whatever was to come seemed good.

And then Peter sensed something odd happening around them. It was becoming evident to him that he and Revealael were being enveloped in swirling vapors of gray, and then black. The clouds grew darker until he could no longer tell where he was. The church, the pew, everything was gone.

The angel pulled him upright and Peter could see nothing beneath his feet. "How strange," he thought, "that I feel as though I am standing upon something, yet, it looks as though there is nothing beneath me but darkness."

Quickly the clouds of darkness dissipated and there was nothing but the darkness itself. That is, except for the light that now seemed to radiate from Revealael.

"Where are we?" asked Peter.

"We are where only angels may go, and of course, the Almighty," he replied. "It is neither specifically here nor there, nor now or then; it simply is."

A small light appeared. It grew and grew in size and Peter was going to ask if the light was actually getting larger or if they were getting closer to it but was distracted from doing so by its ever-increasing beauty.

Soon it became a powerful and majestic display of illumination. It pulsed as though the pulsing was a heartbeat. Yet, looking more closely, the pulsations did not appear to be in any regular pattern. At one time a wave of green would dominate the light and the shade of green would change with each successive pulse of light. Then the pulses of light would be blue one time and yellow the next, maybe followed by red or back to green.

The light was mesmerizing and Peter was sure he had never seen anything so beautiful in his life. Yet, as the source of the light became brighter it did remind him of something he had seen before. What it was he couldn't remember quite yet; for the time being he was too enthralled by the light to do any serious analyzing of it.

Eventually, as it became evident to Peter that they were drawing closer to the source of the light, he could distinguish that there was not one source but several. There seemed to be six individual sources for the light that now nearly enveloped him and the angel. Peacefully encompassing them in its splendor, the beautiful illumination moved in waves that looked like giant curtains of gently flowing colored light.

Traveling outward into infinity, the colorful curtains would sometimes seem to blend together into a beautiful rainbow that was all aglow. Then, at other moments the light would merge and form new shades that would glisten and glow as it passed them with a motion not too unlike the rolling water of a gentle sea.

As the curtains of light continually changed their magnitude, color, and direction, Peter realized that there was one thing about them that remained nearly constant:

each wave of light would bring with it an indescribable feeling of peace and joy.

"What a marvelous place," thought Peter. "This is better than being in the center of a display of fireworks and the northern lights all at the same time. Yes! That's it," it suddenly dawned on him, "this is like the northern lights, only much more powerful and beautiful. It should have come to me before; Revealael said he was an Aurora Angel. That name no doubt relates to the aurora borealis, or northern lights."

Peter thought of that summer night when he was eight years old and had witnessed an exceptionally beautiful display of the aurora borealis with his mother and father. With the flowing curtains of lights shimmering all around as they changed their colors from greens and blues to silver, yellow and tinges of maroon, it was a sight he would never forget.

He remembered how his dad had explained to him that the lights were brought on by sunspot activity affecting the earth, causing ionizations in the upper atmosphere to subsequently release photons of light, or something to that effect. He hadn't totally understood it then either, but he knew the aurora were beautiful, almost beyond the point of description. But these Aurora were incomparably more beautiful.

He finally built up the courage to ask, "Are these lights the reason you're called an Aurora Angel?"

"Yes. They are from the other Aurora Angels," explained Revealael.

"They're marvelous. I've never seen anything close to their beauty. What does it mean?"

"As the Scriptures reveal: 'Creation proclaims the glory of God.' It is the glory of God shinning forth from them."

"So that's how God looks?" questioned Peter, somewhat confused.

"Only in a vague sense. The physical cannot but begin to see the spiritual. The Aurora Angels reflect but a small portion of God's glory. Comparing their apparent glory to that of the Lord is somewhat like comparing the light from a match to that of the sun."

"I'm nearly speechless looking at the beauty I now see. If God's glory is so much more awesome than this, how could anyone ever behold it?"

"Now you are beginning to reach understanding," proclaimed the angel. "No human could behold the awesome glory of God and live. Only those whom the Lord Jesus has transformed into total holiness and the holy angels can see the infinite splendor of God."

At first it all seemed to make good sense, but then he realized something was wrong, and asked, "Revealael, you said that you were one of the Aurora Angels. If so, then why is it that God's glory does not shine forth from you?"

"It does at this very moment. It has been hidden from your view so that you will not be distracted. The messenger does not want to interfere with the message."

"Oh, I understand," Peter said slowly as he tried to comprehend the implications of what the angel had said. "But why is it that the Aurora Angels are here in this place, shinning in the empty darkness?"

"As I told you before, you will find that things are often not as they appear. Indeed, there is very much going on here. The Aurora Angels have been called to watch over this place and to insure that those assigned to its darkness remain within their proper bounds. From time to time, as the Almighty wills, they also reveal to mankind the devious plans concocted by those evil inhabitants. It is, in fact, because of where they are now stationed that the glory radiates so profusely."

"Who are they watching?"

"The fallen angels dwell here in the darkness. They have been here from long ago when they made their decision to serve the creature rather than the Creator. But, they have not yet achieved their full destiny of darkness. For now, they experience the pains of hell while they are allowed to roam the earth in search of souls to tempt, overcome in sin, and ultimately drag into the pit of darkness and gloom with them."

"Why does God not simply destroy them?"

"God allows darkness so that the light will be obvious. The Almighty gave angels as well as men the capacity to freely choose good or evil. In doing so He allows them to make their choice and exist within that choice.

"If the world contained only good choices, there would really be no way to separate the wheat from the chaff. Similarly, a man doesn't really appreciate a full stomach until he has experienced hunger; a man does not become thankful for good health until he has experienced sickness or, at least, witnessed sickness in another; and a man is not thankful for a warm fire until he has been first chilled by the cold."

"Are the evil ones, then, as evil as God is good?" questioned Peter.

"Never compare them to the Almighty. The demons should not be thought of as some evil counterparts of God!" Revealael passionately declared.

"The Almighty God is beyond compare! God's nature is beyond all imagination. He is infinite in goodness and glory and majesty. The fallen angels are mere created beings whom have freely chosen their evil disobedience and are not worthy to be compared to God in any way. A fallen angel has become the opposite of a holy angel.

"But enough of all this talk. I will soon show you some of the fruit of the fallen ones' disobedience. You will see for yourself how utterly hopeless is their decrepit condition."

"You are taking me to the devils?"

"Yes, I will take you to their dwelling place and show you of their evil. I will reveal to you some of the many ways in which they have been working in the world."

"Will they not respond to our presence?"

"Do not fear; they will not harm you. In fact, they could not harm us even if they wanted to. Let it be known that the glory of God shines upon His holy angels and no evil can touch or overpower them, so much greater is the power of good over evil. But, as it is, they will not even know that we are watching them."

"How could they not know of your presence, or can you hide your radiance from them as well as me?"

"Even though the glory of God radiates wondrously from His Aurora Angels when they are near this terrible place of death and destruction, it is seen only by those who have eyes to see. The fallen ones, by their own decision, chose sin and darkness over obedience and light. They refused to acknowledge the glorious Kingship of the Almighty and now they cannot see His glory. The awesome sight of God is forever hidden from them—a terror unimaginable to me!

"It is, in fact, very frustrating for the fallen ones to know that they can never see the holy angels unless we reveal ourselves to them. I will cover you as well, and they will never suspect that we have been near them.

"We will now go to what is and what has been. It may be tempting, but do not even concern yourself with the thought of changing anything of what has been. That cannot be done. God, the Almighty, has forbidden it. What has been written in the Lord's Book of Life cannot be changed. Let this be known: Death comes and then the judgment.

"Enough talk for now. It is time to reveal to you some of the many works that the evil ones have performed in their perversion of the world."

CHAPTER 3

The Demon's Dance

As the billowy-black clouds swirled upon them, Peter's mind raced to try and understand all that was happening. Revealael said they would be traveling beyond the Aurora Angels to that mysterious place of deepest darkness. Of course, assuming where they were going could be properly described as a place. Peter was still more than a little confused about that. There was a lot to take in and comprehend all at once.

He knew not what was in store for him, but he was sure that after this experience with an angel his life would never again be the same. For now, though, he understood that he must try to focus on the truths being revealed to him as Revealael had instructed. Later, there would be sufficient time to meditate upon the deeper meaning of what was happening.

In what had probably been only a few moments, the clouds lifted and Peter found himself engulfed in a faint, red glow. For the first time since Revealael had appeared to him, he felt something other than peace and security. Now, in wave after wave, feelings of gloom, despair, and hatred bombarded him.

It was almost overpowering. Peter was ready to scream out for Revealael to make whatever was causing him to feel this way to go away. Then he felt the angel gently squeeze his hand, and the horrible feelings were gone as quickly as they had came.

"How powerful, indeed, must Revealael be," Peter thought, "to make all that pass away with a simple squeeze of his hand."

It was then that Peter realized Revealael was intently watching what appeared to be a flickering motion at some distance in front of them. While he strained to see the source, he began to hear what sounded like voices faintly chanting. Looking back at Revealael he found the angel apparently waiting for his response.

Revealael said not a word, but nodded in the direction of the motion, chanting, and what also seemed to be the source of the red glow. As time passed, he could tell that they were getting closer to it all.

Drawing nearer, it appeared to Peter that the source of the motion was composed of many parts. There was a great multitude of parts, individual, yet, moving in an ordered unison. Like in some sort of a gigantic, slow-moving mixer, traveling round and round in a circular motion. "What strange sight am I viewing?" he thought.

Shortly, he could see to his dismay that the individual parts of this unusual display were made up of a great multitude of beings and it was from them that the red glow emanated. It seemed to come from each and every one. Even though they must have numbered in the thousands, the eerie, red glow appeared to be no brighter in any one direction than the last light of a flickering ember.

Fear filled Peter's heart as they eventually entered the midst of what was a gruesome horde of beings, and he nervously wiped at the perspiration on his forehead with the back of his hand.

Sensing his anxiety, Revealael said, "Fear not, for they cannot harm you nor can they even detect that we are here."

The angel's words were powerful. They calmed him as he slowly took in the truly awful sight, trying his best to understand. These creatures were far more grotesque than anything he could ever have imagined. Their flesh was all scarred and bubbling with puss sacks, as though they had been engulfed in flames.

But that was nothing compared to the gestures of agony that they made with their faces. Peter would never have believed it possible for anything to be in such agony and yet be alive.

Their facial muscles stretched and contracted in strange contortions as their expression shifted back and forth from what appeared to be physically impossible extremes of movement. And all the changes of expression only seemed to take them slightly away from extreme pain to great pain and back again. Seemingly struggling with every fiber of their being, no matter how hard they tried these monsters were never quite able to free themselves from the grasp of their horror. They were truly a terrible sight.

And, the sound that came forth from them was so horrifying that it made a chill run down his spine until once again he felt the hand of Revealael tighten around his own. Their noise seemed to be somewhere between a chant of agony and a scream of excruciating pain. Though it appeared to vary as an expression of more or less response to pain, it always sounded like a cry of desolate misery.

Still they danced. Round and round and round they went, by the hundreds and the thousands. In a twisted, turning motion that caused Peter to imagine how someone might look while walking on fire. Their bodies would bend over and straighten up as if they had terrible abdominal pains that came and left them in an awful rhythmic sequence. And yet, watching them closely, Peter was sure their agony never left them, not even for a moment.

Through the foul smelling smoke that rose, they continued on their journey in a circle. Around in their strange dance they went, as if they had practiced it forever. In unison they traveled, all the same and ever different. Individual pain and its reaction appeared to be their common cause for dance. Partaking in a mystery of agony, their dance appeared a grotesque progression to some unknown point of pilgrimage.

Finally, Peter had the state of mind to blurt out, "Are these tormented beasts the fallen angels? And why are they dancing?"

"One question at a time," Revealael replied in a voice so calm that it took Peter by surprise. "I will answer all your questions in due time. For now, know that these creatures you see here are the fallen angels. It is these beings to whom the Scriptures speak when they say that a third of the stars fell from heaven. The pitiful beings you now behold were once glorious angels of the Almighty and inhabited the heavenly domain.

"Before the time of man, God created all the angels as beings of free will. But some chose to look inward and rebelled, saying, 'Truly we are glorious in majesty and might. None is superior to us. Who can oppose our will?' They made the decision to serve themselves rather than the Creator and thus lost their glory and much of their power.

"You should know that the result of their sin is not totally like that of mortal man's. You of the family of man have a limited understanding and so by the grace of God are allowed to repent and conform your lives to His will. The angels were given immortality and much more knowledge and understanding and so their decision to obey or disobey was necessarily indissoluble. Once an angel decided to follow either God or self, there could be no changing of their course.

"It is somewhat like the Scripture in which we find that those who are given more will have more expected of them. The angels have been given much and thus their very nature demands a very different response than is expected or possible from man.

"Now there is no choice for them. The fallen angels could no more become obedient than the holy angels could disobey God. We are not like you. We are not creatures bound by time. Our decisions are always present. You must come to understand that it is impossible for the fallen angels to repent."

"Why do they dance?" Peter asked, shaking his head.

"They are experiencing what we call the 'Dance of Distraction.' They can never experience anything close to what you would call joy, but, even in their agony, they think that they have cause for celebration. They believe that they have won a great victory and so they do this. The dance expresses the slight distraction that they are now experiencing from their pain and anguish. I will tell you more of this, but first, you must see something else."

And the black swirling clouds moved in again. In but a moment, an opening appeared and Peter was led through the portal by Revealael into a totally different world.

This new destination was not at all like the confusing and depressed place that they had just left; it was peaceful and beautiful with lush vegetation everywhere. Peter could feel the warm rays of the sun. It was indeed a welcome stop in, what was for Peter, the middle of a harsh winter.

And the refreshing air—the sweet, clean air—was everywhere. He turned his head in one direction and then the other, just trying to take in as much of the sights and smells as possible. Flowers could be seen all around, and their tantalizing fragrance brought a joy to his heart.

"There must be ripe muskmelon nearby," Peter thought, picking up the distinctive aroma in the air. For a second it reminded him of his dad's garden; it was there where he first encountered those luscious fruits. "Dad's garden couldn't hold a candle to this place, though," he mused.

Everywhere he looked there was something growing that was good to eat. To the left were grapevines with extraordinarily large dark purple fruits hanging in huge clusters. When he looked to his right he could see a clearing full of strawberry plants that were loaded with berries nearly the size of chicken eggs.

As Revealael led him by the hand up a small hill, the sight overwhelmed Peter. Everywhere he looked he saw a marvelous display of creation. In the sky was a myriad of beautifully colored birds, and the air was gently filled with their singing. As they passed through a thick blanket of grass, the thought passed through Peter's mind that he could well lay there for days absorbing all the sights, smells, and sounds. "Surely," he thought, "this is the most marvelous garden ever!"

Reaching the crest of the hill, Peter was surprised to find two people. A man and a woman were lying in the tall grass a short distance below. Beside them they had several of the clumps of luscious grapes. Between them was a large leaf that looked like the ear of an elephant, and it was heaped full of strawberries and blueberries.

The pair were casually feeding themselves, and sometimes each other, with the fruit as they lay upon their backs, apparently watching the fluffy snow-white clouds that were high up in the air drift slowly by.

Peter thought, "How fortunate these people are to live in this place." Turning to Revealael he asked, "Who are these people and where are we?"

"They are Adam and Eve, your original parents, and we are in the Garden of Eden," replied the angel.

"You mean we are actually seeing the world right after the creation?"

"Yes, but that is not exactly what I said. I said that we are there, and so we are. You know how I told you that time has no effect on God, well it doesn't. We have been allowed to pass through a doorway, so to speak, and are now actually in the Garden with your first parents."

"But they don't seem to notice us," Peter quipped, not quite prepared to accept what had happened to him.

"They cannot see us," reassured Revealael. "The Almighty will not allow what has happened to be changed in the slightest, not even by our being seen. God has given man the capability to choose good or evil and He will not allow man's decisions to be revoked.

"God's grace is constantly at work trying to move the hearts of men so they may come to Him. He has poured out His love on all of mankind. But, he forces no one to do good, or to sin."

"This world is so beautiful and perfect, Revealael, I can't imagine why anyone would ever feel the need to do anything wrong."

"This is a perfect world. Anything good that man could ever want or imagine can be found here. In fact, the whole universe lies before man for his enjoyment. There would never be hunger, cold or lack of companionship, and the peace and joy of living in the Almighty's grace would forever flow through the heart of man. This is Paradise."

Suddenly, the black clouds rolled in, and everything disappeared from view. It was an unwilling passage. In his heart Peter wanted to stay in Paradise.

No sooner had they entered when another portal appeared, and Peter was lead quickly through it by Revealael. It was a world so brightly lit that Peter had to almost totally close his eyes in order to see. The sun shone down hot and hard in this near desert world they had entered.

A strong wind blew sand in Peter's face until it pained him. If he had previously held feelings that had questioned whether he was really present here in the past, they quickly faded.

"What a harsh world," Peter mumbled as he gazed around, half squinting from the sunlight and half from trying to keep the sand out of his eyes. "Where are we?" he shouted over the roar of the wind.

"This is nearly the same place and time as we just left. Not much different, yet, everything has changed!" proclaimed the angel with a look and voice that Peter realized was no different in this environment than it had previously been.

Revealael seemed oblivious to the harshness around them, and he pointed toward a clump of bushes several yards away, and began walking in that direction. As they drew closer, Peter could see that there was a man and a woman lying within, seeking shelter from the storm.

Yes, it was the same man and woman from the garden. Now, though, Adam and Eve looked much different. Their peaceful contented looks were gone. The man lie face down on the ground slowly hitting it with his fist. He seemed in agony as he murmured something.

The woman lie curled up in a ball, sobbing pitiably and clawing her abdomen with her long slender nails as though thinking that the physical pain she was bringing upon herself somehow could ease the obvious pain that she was experiencing on the inside. Peter wondered if she was trying to hurt herself or if she somehow thought that by defacing what God had made that she was hurting God.

He felt sorry for the man and woman. Their external world had been changed immensely, but how much more was their world changed on the inside. What emptiness must be within them. What loneliness and fear must they feel in this harsh place separated from God. What a change, to be God's friend one day, living in His grace and be alienated to Him, through sin, the next. No wonder they were in such anguish.

Before he could get his mind off his languishing ancestors, Peter found himself within the dark pathways of time. As he was led into the place of the dull, red glow, he could again hear the rhythmic chanting of the living-dead as they moaned over and over their hopeless song of pain.

Around and around and around they went, in unison, yet different. Like waves upon the ocean, they were dissimilar yet moving all together. In their eerie, tortured movements one could from time to time almost imagine a fleeting glimpse of their distraction as they endured their gruesome dance in a never ending cycle.

"Why have we returned to this awful place of the demons?" questioned Peter.

"We are here because you must come to understand the role that the demons play in the affairs of mankind," answered Revealael.

"The dance that you see the demons doing could be called their victory celebration. They have played a large part in causing the fall of man from God's grace and so they celebrate. Although, it is more accurately defined as a slight distraction from pain than a celebration in any sense of the word that you have known.

"Winning souls for the kingdom of darkness causes the demons to concentrate on those fallen people's misery and eternal loss, allowing them to ever so slightly be distracted from their own misery and pain. It seems a small point to you and I, but for them, destined to an eternal separation from God and an eternity in hell, any distraction from their misery is worth every effort. And so, they diligently work to get and keep mankind away from the grace of God.

"That is why we call their fruitless action, 'The Dance of Distraction.' It is not bringing to them any real sort of fulfillment or relief that one could acknowledge, only a slight distraction from pain.

"Throughout mankind's history there are always small groups doing the dance for souls they have conquered. Only at select times throughout history have they considered themselves to have won such a great victory that they all dance to the same distraction as you see here.

"Truly, the fall of your first parents from the grace of God was a monumental point in time. It has, in fact, defined all the rest of human history. As you know, their fall from grace not only affected them but also their children down through the ages. Their progeny has been born outside the grace of God.

"Because of this the demons feel they have captured the victory, a victory before the game has hardly begun. Their present dance is in anticipation of all the lost souls who will be joining them in eternal misery.

"From their perspective there is much additional suffering and pain to anticipate. Their leader, Lucifer, was instrumental in causing Adam and Eve to disobey God and commit the original human sin. Lucifer convinced them to doubt, question, and disobey the Word of God, and so they did. After seeing the effectiveness of this approach, you can be sure the demons will continue to use it as their main plan of attack throughout all of history.

"Never forget; the demons are evil but they are not stupid. Magnificent creations of the Almighty, they freely chose the path of disobedience and evil. They have incredible intelligence and power compared to mortal man. How skillful they are at perverting God's Word in what may at times seem to be a minute way, so that its meaning will lead to death rather than eternal life with Our Lord, who is blessed and glorious forever.

"But come, this is only the beginning of what I have been sent to show you. There is much more that you need to understand. Let us then proceed. The time is near when it will be too late for those who need to hear the truth to respond to it. Now is the time to act."

AURORA ANGELS

CHAPTER 4

Ancient Days

The darkness engulfed them only for a moment, and then, as Peter had come to expect, the portal appeared. As they stepped into this new place and time, he felt his heart race in anticipation of the scene he would see.

There before them crouched a man flailing his arm wildly into the tall grass. He wore only a short skirt that appeared to be made of sheepskin or deerskin. Exposing much body hair, Peter thought he rather resembled some sort of wild ape-man.

And he acted like an animal in terror. With his eyes bulging out of his head, he glared, first in one direction and then the other like he was afraid someone might find him.

As Peter drew nearer, he understood what the half-crazy man was doing. He was trying to wipe something off of his hands and arms, something he obviously did not want anyone to see.

It didn't take Peter long to realize what it was. Deep red blotches of blood were splattered all over him.

"Yes, that's it," thought Peter, as a cringe of fear ran through his body. "He must have killed someone and now he is trying to remove the evidence."

Flashes of lightning appeared overhead and loud booms of thunder followed. With them a strong wind caused dark clouds to speed across the sky. Seeing this, a feeling of doom descended upon Peter. It seemed as though nature itself had been prompted to proclaim to the grave seriousness of what this man had done.

Noticing sadness on the face of Revealael for the first time, Peter asked him, "Why do you look so sad? Who is this man, and whom has he killed?"

"You behold the first-born of Adam and Eve. This is Cain and he has just killed his brother, Abel. He realizes the seriousness of his awful crime and attempts to remove the blood of his brother that is upon him."

"I've never really understood why he killed him," confessed Peter.

"He killed Abel because of jealousy," revealed the angel. "His brother had something that he did not have—God's favor. For those who are willing to see, it is already evident that the original sin of Adam and Eve is having a profound effect upon mankind. Man's separation from God is very sad."

"Yes," Peter interjected, nodding his head in agreement, "but what was it that brought Abel into favor with God and caused Cain to become so jealous of him?"

"Man looks at the outward appearances; God looks to the heart. Cain had a self-serving heart that was cold to God. He wanted the benefit of saying that his life was good and pleasing to God without actually doing that which pleased God. But, man cannot fool the Almighty!

"Cain knew full well what it was that God wanted. He knew of the Word of God which had been spoken to his parents, but he preferred to twist what God wanted into something that would fit into his lifestyle. It is all so very common. Man tries to conform the Word of God to fit into what he wants rather than letting God's Word stand as it is and thus transform man.

"God clearly told Adam after the fall that in his time 'cursed is the ground because of you.' Yet, Cain had the audacity to bring that, which had come out of the ground, to God as an offering. Cain ignored the Word of God and followed a course of action that he deemed best rather than do what God wanted and so as the Scriptures say, God had no regard for Cain and his offering.

"Therefore in his jealous anger, Cain plotted and killed his brother, Abel, to whom God had shown high regard. Man's ways of death and destruction started at the beginning and follow through the course of history to your own time. The scene of Cain killing his brother has been repeated over and over again down through the ages. This is the destiny for sinful man. It is exactly what the Scripture attests to when it says, 'Then desire when it has conceived gives birth to sin; and sin when it is full-grown brings forth death.'

"This all came about because of the original sin of your first parents. This sin affects all who are born into the world. It does not cause problems on just a small scale. I will show you."

Before Peter could say a word, the black clouds came in the same manner as before. He was glad that they were going somewhere else and could no longer see the pathetic sight of the man who had committed murder. And thinking about it for a moment, he realized that what had happened there was really no different than what happens every time someone is murdered—man kills his brother!

Peter found himself being lead through a portal in the dark clouds. They were standing in the air, hovering a hundred feet or so above a surface of water in the midst of a terrific storm. The rain poured down harder with each passing moment.

As the lightning and thunder came at them from every direction, Peter thought it was like being in the middle of some fierce battle with cannons going off all around them.

At first, since there was no land in sight, Peter thought they were positioned over an ocean or sea. Then, straining to look through the driving rain, he saw a hillside in the distance. As Revealael brought them closer, he realized the magnitude of this rainfall. Looking down into the depth of water, Peter saw the roof of someone's dwelling.

Drawing ever nearer, Peter could see farther up the hillside where there was a large group of people struggling with their belongings, trying to reach the higher ground. Some had wagons and some had sleds that were being pulled by oxen and horses, and there was even one wagon being pulled by three men. One thing they seemed to have in common, though, was that they were all frantic in their struggle to reach safety.

After gazing upon this scene for a moment, he could see why they were frantically racing up the hill. The water level was ascending so rapidly that its distance from them was quickly decreasing in spite of their efforts to outrun it.

Huge waves were beginning to buffet the hill, and before any of the people below had time to see them coming, three wagons and a dozen people with their animals were swept into the raging waters. The remaining people panicked, dropped everything they had, and began running for the top of the hill.

It was to no avail. Within moments the waves swept away all the remaining souls as they lapped the very crest of the hill. Soon nothing but water could be seen.

They were moving again, but try as he may, Peter did not spot anything solid until he had searched for quite some time. Finally, at a great distance, he found an object floating upon the water. He could eventually see it was a large boat that was gently rolling with the waves. Like a cross between a barn and a ship, it was a mammoth ark.

"Is that what I think it is?" Peter excitedly blurted out. "Is that Noah's Ark?"

"Yes it is," replied the angel with a resolve that made Peter realize that what he was about to say was very important. "Within that ark is Noah, his family, and all the animals of the land and air which are destined to repopulate the face of the earth."

"Then the story of the flood is true. It is not just some metaphor?" questioned Peter, turning his head away from the ark to see the reaction of the angel.

"God's Word is true; it does not mislead," proclaimed Revealael forcefully. "How presumptuous, indeed, is man in your day to think that if he cannot understand something then it could not have happened.

"The ways and the thoughts of the Almighty are as high above man as the heavens are above the earth. If God could make the earth and all the heavens in which it resides with a 'Word,' then surely He would have no trouble doing something so simple as making the waters of the earth rise to entirely flood the world.

"This is not a new problem for man though. Being presumptuous has much to do with why God is destroying the people of the world here in Noah's time. Hearts have truly grown cold and hard since the days of Adam and Eve. Wickedness and death reached a level that God would no longer tolerate, and so He almost totally wiped mankind from the face of the earth.

"In his heart man said, 'Where is God? He will not show his face and so I will do what I deem to be right.'

"Therefore, the earth was full of every evil. The original sin that brought spiritual death to Adam, Eve and their descendants reached maturity in their depravation and the treatment of man towards man.

"It's no different than in my time, is it?" asked Peter

"No, but, be not discouraged by the sinful acts of men. God allows sin so that the futility of life without God will become evident to all, causing at least some to come to repentance and be saved from the jaws of eternal death.

"Now, above all, remember the vision of the Ark that you see before you on the waters. There is great significance here for what is to come. The waters symbolize the waters of baptism through which man may be saved. The Ark symbolizes the vehicle—the Church."

"Yes," thought Peter, "I never really thought of it that way but it does make perfect sense now."

Before he could think about it any further, the dark passageway of time was upon them and a doorway was opening into a new revelation for Peter. And once again a familiar scene appeared.

Still they circled round in their endless tortured motion. In agony and pain they danced in their horrific celebration. Their chanting reached a fever pitch before suddenly it all ceased into an eerie silence.

"You idiotic fools!" screamed a piercing voice from the very center of what was now a totally motionless mass of sickening creatures, causing a chill to run all the way down to the tips of Peter's toes. "How can you dance here while some of them are getting away? You did not get them all. We must have every last one of their putrid, miserable souls and then we can truly celebrate our distraction! Get to work or I swear by the darkness that I will have each and every one of you for my distraction!"

With that, the disgusting multitude broke out in a terrible scream and then dissipated off into every direction until there was none left but the one who had spoken.

Hideous indeed was he. With a head that had two faces, four stout legs, a long, thick tail, and deep, burnt-red hide that appeared like one might expect the thoroughly roasted hide of an alligator to look.

The hideous creature raised his one front leg, made a fist with its claw of a hand, and shaking it in the air screamed with a demented howl, "All! I shall have them all! And they will know that I am lord!"

Peter knew who this creature was, but he was about to confirm his thought when the angel said, "Now that you have seen Lucifer's arrogance and pride it should be apparent why he would not submit to the Almighty."

Peter shook his head in understanding, though he was still taken aback by what he had just witnessed. At the moment he was even more amazed at Revealael and the rock-solid confidence expressed in his voice and the look of determination on his face. Revealael was obviously not the slightest bit intimidated or afraid of this creature, Lucifer.

With a confidence so strong that it forced the fear right out of Peter's heart, Revealael proclaimed, "And now, I will show you more of the treacherous ways in which these masters of evil work. Rest assured, in the end their ways will be known to all and their defeat manifested to every eye. Our Lord and God shall reign triumphantly!"

Again, the dark clouds appeared and when Peter could see out from within their confines a new age was revealed. It looked like a marvelous age for man, as a wondrous city lay before him that would have made any age proud. In the center of the city, he could see a tower that appeared to reach upward to the highest clouds in the sky. Peter had seen the tall skyscrapers of New York City but they were no comparison for this tower either in height or beauty.

At first glance, everything seemed to be fine, but then Peter noticed, as he looked down from their perspective some several hundred feet in the air above, that the traffic was all departing the city.

Small groups were leaving in every direction. With their possessions in carts and wagons, tied to animals, and strapped on their backs, Peter was reminded of the futile fleeing to high ground of the inhabitants that he had witnessed at the time of the Great Flood. This time, though, there was no rising water.

Turning to look at Revealael he asked, "Who are these people and why are they all leaving this magnificent city?"

"They are considered to be the elite people of this age. They gathered here to build this city as an example to their world and all time of their great ability and wisdom. That tower is their crowning attestation to the glory of man. Today was the day of its dedication.

"These people served and glorified the creature rather than the Great Creator. The Almighty humbled them by removing from their minds part of the gift of intelligence that He had given them. But by a word of command, they no longer have the ability to understand the language of each other. Now they cannot work together and become powerful. They will scatter in small bands to the four corners of the earth where it will be much harder for them to progress further in their glorification of man."

"What is the proper purpose for man in this world?" asked Peter, somewhat confused at exactly what it was that a man should strive for in life.

"There is absolutely nothing in this life that is important except that which helps mankind to know, love and serve the Almighty," said the angel. "All else is vanity. When a man puts himself at the center of his universe, there is no room for God.

"Be aware, Peter, that the basic scene that you are now seeing will be repeated over and over again throughout history. Every time men turn away from God and His ways and seek to follow the so-called wisdom of the world, the civilization that those men have become so proud of will be destroyed."

Caught up in the moment and not really thinking about what he was saying, Peter asked, "Is there then no real hope for man's future?"

"Yes, Peter, there surely is. Not in man's works though. Man's environmental condition and his worldly achievements count for little. It is the spiritual condition of man that is of long-lasting significance. True happiness comes only through the grace of God. Only in God is the soul at rest!"

"What must people do to please God and find happiness?" inquired Peter.

"Enough talk. I will show you the way to please the Almighty."

No sooner had Revealael spoken than Peter found himself in the midst of time's dark mystery. When the portal opened they stepped through to a near face to face encounter with a man standing above a boy who was tied up and lying on a large rock.

The man held in his right hand a long knife as tears streamed down his face. He had a look of consternation that said to Peter that this man was about to do something that he really did not want to do.

Peter flinched as he saw the powerful muscles in the arm of the man flex and he quickly began to raise the knife. But before the man could plunge the knife downward a loud booming voice was heard from above, "Abraham, Abraham!"

And the man said, "Here am I."

Then the voice from above declared, "Do not lay your hand on the lad or do anything to him; for now I know that you fear God, seeing you have not withheld your son, your only son, from me."

Peter whispered to Revealael, "Is that God's voice?"

"In a sense," replied Revealael. "His angel has been sent to speak for Him. To see this is why I have brought you here. Abraham has proven his faith in the Almighty this day and all generations of faith-filled people will look to him as their father.

"What Abraham was asked to do was not easy for him. It was very hard. He had waited many years for a son. Then, God asked him to sacrifice his only son. It was a very difficult command for him to obey. But, he trusted totally in God and looked to the future, realizing that without God man has nothing. Abraham obeyed and demonstrated his faith in God.

"God wants all people to have faith like the kind that Abraham has. The faith he wants is a living faith that puts the will of God first in a person's life. Having faith in God means living for Him. Just believing that God exists is not faith. As the Scriptures attest, even the demons believe that God exists, and they tremble.

"Faith in God means that a person is willing to step out and do what God asks. This is what God demands of every man and woman. Without faith it is impossible to please God. Do you believe this?"

"Oh, yes... yes I do believe," answered Peter. "I have no problem with that at all."

"That is very good," reassured the angel as he broadly smiled.

"But isn't more than even faith necessary to make things right with God?"

"You have spoken well, Peter," answered Revealael. "Although, I still have much more to show you."

AURORA ANGELS

CHAPTER 5

The Plan Unfolds

Again within the swirling black clouds, Peter eagerly awaited the familiar sight of the portal. In a few moments he was led through that doorway of time into a new, yet old, world.

"Behold," boomed the voice of his angelic companion, "the power of God!"

From his vantage point, hovering a hundred feet or so in the air, Peter could see a vast armada of people traveling with horses; oxen; sheep; and goats; and every sort of animal along with their children and all their possessions. In carts, in sleds, and loaded upon their backs, thousands upon thousands were hastily carrying their belongings to a new destination.

Peter soon understood the reason for their speedy migration. Just a short distance behind them came a rapidly approaching army. Whether on horseback or with chariot, the pursuers' fierce determination was evident as they cracked their whips wildly, hastening to the full extent of their steed's ability the impending encounter.

"It looks like this battle will be quite one-sided," said Peter to the angel who did not respond. "The horsemen and charioteers are well armed with swords and spears while the multitude they chase carry nothing but staffs and hoes."

But, it was not until after watching for awhile that Peter noticed the setting for this great race to disaster was upon the dry bed of a sea. The waters on each side of the fleeing multitude had been driven back, causing a very precarious situation. Two gigantic walls of water straddled those fleeing.

When it appeared that only a few minutes remained before the slaughter, the last of the pursued reached the eastern bank of the sea. Then, Peter noticed a man raise his hand and the walls of water returned to their natural placement with a roar. Within the violent rush of water, the pursuing army was swept away into the grasp of death.

Only after all this did Revealael speak. "See, once again God saves his people through water. Those who trust in Him have found salvation through the power of God manifested in the saving waters. The unbelievers have found death and condemnation through those same waters."

Pointing towards those who were safely on dry land, Peter asked, "These are the Hebrews who have been in bondage in the land of Egypt, aren't they? Moses has just led them through the Sea of Reeds and is taking them on their journey to the Promised Land."

"Yes," Revealael agreed. "It is through Moses that God will give them the Ten Commandments while they are on their journey. These laws will bring illumination to the world as has never before been seen. It is these very same Commandments that have become the basis for the laws of most of the societies throughout the world. They have profoundly enlightened mankind."

"But just obeying the Commandments won't make everything right, will it?" asked Peter.

"You are most correct," replied Revealael. "Obeying the Commandments is good and pleasing to God, but that is not enough. That in itself does not have the power to bridge the great abyss that separates mankind from God that was formed by original sin.

"The Commandments point out very significant actions that are either acceptable or unacceptable to God. They help a person think correctly about God, their neighbor, and the world in general. Most importantly, the Commandments point out the actual sin in a person's life so that he may repent, turn to God, and be open to all the graces that God wants to give him.

"One of the demons' greatest victories has been to convince people, including many within the Church, not to speak about sin. This is a great injustice. Without the knowledge of what sinful acts are, a person cannot come to repentance and thus unto the grace of God!"

"Yes," said Peter, "I have many times heard that we should not be 'judgmental' and speak of sin. People quote Jesus saying, 'Judge not least ye be judged.' "

"That Scripture is greatly abused," the angel forcefully replied, "Christians are the mouth of Christ in the world; if they don't speak the truth of Christ then it will not be made known. The Scriptures reveal that Christians are to not judge unjustly, but they are certainly called to justly judge actions. Speaking out about sin in a just manner is part of being a light to the world. But one can only judge actions correctly if one uses the proper yardstick, and that is the Word of God.

"Revealing the Word of God is good, holy, and proper. Although, one must always remember to love the sinner while pointing out the sin. Still, serious sin should never be overlooked for fear of offending the sinner. Let me now show you, Peter, the great good that can come from being faced with one's sin."

Time's darkness came, and time did not remain as it had been. Swirling seemingly aimless but for a moment, black clouds gave way to Revealael's will, and the portal was revealed. Peter and the angel stepped out into a new time and place and revelation.

There before Peter lay a man prostate upon the bare ground. He was all dressed in sackcloth and unkempt as though he had been in mourning for many days. Peter could hear him praying and, though the words could not all be understood, he could from time to time hear him say, "I am unworthy."

As they drew closer, Peter could see that the man had been sorrowful to the point of shedding tears as the dark stain of dirt from beneath his eyes attested to their moisture which had mixed with the earth's dust. Obviously this man was of some great importance, as several servants dressed in fine clothing stood around him waiting for a beckoning from him—a call the man seemed not interested in making.

"Do you know whom this man is," queried Revealael, "and why he is down upon the ground in prayer?"

"No! But please tell me," answered Peter without at all understanding what he was viewing.

"This is David, the king. Before you is he whom God would call a man after His own heart. It is he who, when but a boy, with his hands slew both lion and bear. It is he who won victory for his people by killing the giant Goliath with but a pebble. It was he who united his people and brought the Ark of the Covenant to Jerusalem.

"This same King David grieved the Lord greatly when he arranged for the death of Uriah to hide the sin he had committed with Uriah's wife, Bathsheba. And, he would have remained in sin had not the prophet Nathan fearlessly come to him with the Word of God, making David face up to his sin so he might therefore repent.

"David is a man with a very good heart. He wants to do the will of God, that he may please the Almighty. As all men, he has great weaknesses within him due to the effects of original sin. He made some very bad decisions, but he now admits his sin.

"It can greatly help a person to avoid sin if he realizes the forces that are at work in his life. Prayer is needed. Man cannot do right without God's help. The flesh of man has a tendency that lures him into all sorts of sin, but the flesh is not the greatest foe of man.

"The greatest battle for man is not flesh and blood but is the evil powers within the world—the demons. Man cannot win this battle without God's help. I will show you."

Darkness came but for a mere moment. Before Peter realized anything was happening, he found that he and Revealael were standing atop a huge building.

"Where are we now?" he asked in bewilderment.

"We are atop of King David's palace on the day he looked down and saw Bathsheba bathing and had her brought to him. There was more at work here than just the actions of David and Bathsheba. Powerful forces were at work, pushing them into the direction of sin. I will open your eyes to the fullness of what happened here this day so that you may see and believe."

The image of two semi-transparent beings appeared. Surveying the palace area, they seemed more like shadows than real beings, so elusive was their presence. Peter knew, from his observations of hell, that these were demons. Had he not known, he soon could have figured it out from the conversation that he was about to overhear.

"You know what our master told us," said the one. "We must be very shrewd with this David."

"Yes," said the other. "The Messiah that is to come will spring forth from his lineage. If we can get David alienated from his God we can foil his God's plan."

"You know what we should do," continued the first. "We must convince David to walk about the palace and also convince the woman, Bathsheba that it is all right to go out and bathe early in the day."

"Right," replied the other, "one step at a time. Once we have gotten David to see her we can get him to lust in his heart for her and then I'm sure we can convince him that he deserves to lay with her."

"I know we can," said the first. "We will trip him up on his strong point. He is a very passionate person. He is passionate in his love for his God, but I am sure that his passion can also be used against him.

"If we keep our sights fixed upon the final outcome we can convince him that it is right for him to do what we want. He is no match for our power. He is but a weak mortal."

"Yes, yes!" said the other. "It's easy to get these mortals to come up with a self-righteous excuse for their actions."

"It's so easy that it is almost not worth the trouble," said the first, as he was joined by the other demon in a laugh that was as evil as his appearance. "Let's be at it now. You work at Bathsheba and I'll take on David."

At that point, Peter experienced the darkness roll in, and then he and Revealael were back to the time where they witnessed King David in sackcloth lying before them on the ground.

Breaking the silence, Revealael said, "See before you a man who is now broken in spirit but who will be healed by

The Plan Unfolds

the Lord and go forth to be a great servant of the Almighty. Before you is the man to whose lineage the Messiah will be pleased to be born.

"Never forget this example. Nathan would not have favored David by ignoring his sin. God's love is always manifested in truth."

"You spoke of the Messiah," responded Peter excitedly as he thought he could see in what direction his instruction from Revealael was headed. "There could not be reconciliation to the Father without His entrance into the world, could there?"

"True. You are most correct," answered Revealael. "All the repentance in the world would have accomplished naught if the Savior had not come into the world. At the appointed time came the Messiah to set mankind free from the grasp of sin and death. He came so that all who would believe and follow Him could be led to the Father.

"Without the Messiah there would be no forgiveness of sin. His death made reconciliation to the Father possible. As the Word says, 'Without the shedding of blood there is no forgiveness.' Only the blood of the Messiah would be worthy to wash away the sin of the world. But first, in the fullness of time, man had to come to an understanding of sin and repentance.

"All did not welcome the Messiah. The truth is not always pleasantly received. Not many were prepared to repent. He was not the kind of Messiah they were prepared for or had envisioned. Many expected the Savior to free them from the Romans and bring prosperity to their land. Others sought a Messiah who would be a King of kings upon the earth, ruling all the nations. Most still did not recognize the great sinfulness of their lives, and so they did not acknowledge their need for One to save them from sin.

They most surely did not look for or want a Suffering Servant. They thought of the physical, not the spiritual.

"They were looking for a lion, yet He came as a lamb. They wanted freedom from the world, but He came to free them from sin. They looked for Him to bring something to them; instead, He came to bring them to Someone—His Father."

CHAPTER 6

Salvation or Desolation

The tapestry of time descended, engulfing them within its darkness. When the portal appeared, Peter and the angel stepped through to find themselves standing upon a beautiful hillside. The warm air carried the sweet fragrance of wild flowers as it whisked a few fluffy clouds peacefully across the sky.

They were not alone. A crowd was quickly gathering. Ever larger by the moment, its size increased by twos, threes, and fours, as people young and old hastened up the winding trails to this hillside pasture. They came until there must have been several thousand.

After watching the movement of the crowd up the hill for several minutes, Peter did not understand their purpose for gathering any more than in the beginning and so he turned toward Revealael for an explanation. He found the angel smiling down at him, waiting in anticipation of his question.

"Wait a little longer and you will have your answer, and much more," came the response.

It was then that Peter noticed that the people were all beginning to stop what they were doing and began turning their attention up the hill. He, too, gazed toward the top, about a hundred yards away, and saw what seemed at first to be a sunbeam striking a group of men who were on the crest of the hill. After closer examination it appeared the glow was somehow coming from within the group of men.

Suddenly, all the noise of the gathering throng stopped, even the birds were silent, and it became so quiet that one could have heard a leaf fall from a tree as a man sitting amongst the group on the hilltop began to speak. It was as if all creation had paused to hear the message that this man would give.

In a voice that was soft, yet saturated the hillside the man proclaimed, "Blessed are the poor in spirit for theirs is the kingdom of heaven. Blessed are they that mourn for they shall be comforted. Blessed are the meek for they shall inherit the earth. Blessed are they who do hunger and thirst after righteousness for they shall be filled. Blessed are the merciful for they shall obtain mercy. Blessed are the pure in heart for they shall see God."

"Jesus! That's Jesus!" Peter exclaimed aloud, in a voice that would have brought attention to himself from probably half the people who were gathered there, had they been able to hear him.

Peter knew that no one but Revealael could hear his outburst, but still, he began to show some sign of embarrassment as his face turned red.

"That is all right," assured the angel in his usual confident and calming voice. "Our talking will not bother anyone. If the people here realized just whom it was that was speaking to them they too would become so excited that they would shout out His name. It is indeed a great privilege to be in this place and hear the Lord of lords and King of kings teaching."

"Yes, thank you for bringing me here," whispered Peter excitedly. "It is wonderful to be standing here listening to Jesus. I cannot believe this is happening."

"Thank God," Revealael gently corrected him. "From the Almighty does all grace and blessings flow. Savor these moments because they are exceedingly marvelous."

Turning his attention toward the hilltop, Peter could hear Jesus saying, "Think not that I am come to destroy the law, or the prophets: I am not come to destroy, but to fulfill. For verily I say unto you, Till heaven and earth pass, one jot or one title shall in no wise pass from the law, till all be fulfilled. Whosoever therefore shall break one of these least commandments, and shall teach men so, he shall be called the least in the kingdom of heaven but whosoever shall do and teach them, the same shall be called great in the kingdom of heaven."

"The words that Jesus is speaking are exactly as they are recorded in the Bible, aren't they?" asked Peter sounding somewhat relieved.

"Yes!" answered the angel. "I can assure you that the Aramaic that Jesus now speaks is exactly the words of the original text of the Holy Bible. Does that surprise you?"

"No, it is just that there are so many so-called experts who claim that what the Bible says is not what Jesus meant that it is reassuring to hear Him proclaim these words. Some people seem to think God could make a mistake and that He could not express Himself in words that would last for all time.

"What really amazes me," Peter continued, "is that the experts can read Jesus' warning about not teaching contrary to His Word and then do that very thing! It would seem that of all people they would be most cautious not to pervert the Word of God."

Revealael nodded approvingly, saying, "You have spoken well Peter. Pride dwelling in the heart of man, is a powerful weapon for the enemy to use against the kingdom. This is why our Lord has spoken these words and why they are recorded for all generations."

"A thought just occurred to me," Peter said curiously. "If Jesus is speaking in Aramaic, then how is it that I am hearing Him in English?"

Doing something that Peter had not previously witnessed, Revealael laughed out loud as he said, "If that one small miracle has impressed you so much, you will indeed be amazed when you reflect back on all that has and will happen."

Focusing his attention back toward Jesus, Peter noticed that the crowd was held spellbound by His words. They marveled at someone speaking with such conviction and authority. Truly, this man was teaching as though He understood what He spoke of by first-hand knowledge and not just on a theoretical level as their rabbis did.

Peter also was caught up in the message. It was more than the words. It was even more than the way that He said them. Although, that in itself was extremely moving. Jesus had a manner that reached out and touched a person. It was as though He was speaking directly to each and every person individually. Peter thought that maybe He was. After all, this was no ordinary man; this was the Lord of Creation.

Enraptured by the words of the Messiah, he listened intently, and after some time Jesus said, "Not every one that saith unto me, Lord, Lord, shall enter into the kingdom of heaven. Many will say to me in that day, Lord, Lord, have we not prophesied in thy name? and in thy name have cast out devils? and in thy name done many wonderful works? And then will I profess unto them, I never knew you depart from me, ye that work iniquity."

Peter found himself joining the crowd in gasping at those words. He knew better. He was simply caught up in the moment. He knew well enough that it was not lip service that God desired, but a commitment to obey His will. And it was not a new concept; the idea that God wanted His followers to have an active faith had been known at least as far back as their father Abraham's time.

What a joy to hear the Messiah speak. No one had ever spoken with such authority and captivating wisdom as He. Peter was finding out that the Lord could make anything that He spoke about seem crystal clear.

It was as though speech and understanding were both under the command of Jesus. It was as though His words were an extension of His Being. As Peter thought about it he realized that they, of course, were.

There was no time now to meditate on all these things; Jesus had finished speaking and was moving through the crowd. He was coming down the hill in the general direction of Peter and Revealael. Peter's heart raced in anticipation of being so close to the Lord.

The crowd that had been amazingly quiet while Jesus spoke was now going wild. They were pressing in on Him, trying to see Jesus up close, to speak to Him, or to touch Him. It seemed that everyone in the crowd had decided to request something of Him.

And then, as though on cue, words were shouted over and over by the crowd. They radiated outward from the area around Jesus, as ripples from a stone thrown in a pond.

"He healed the leper! He healed the leper!" went out the cry from the crowd, and a poor, ragged man could be seen jumping up and down near Jesus.

Such was the excitement that Peter thought he would not have been surprised if the very trees on the hillside began to shout their praise. He could see the man running excitedly from one person to the other showing them the hands and arms and face that had only moments before been eaten raw by a cruel disease. Now they were as beautiful, clear, and smooth as a newborn's flesh.

"How truly wonderful it is to be here, " thought Peter. But he had not much time to think of that, because he could see that Jesus and the entourage around Him were headed directly towards him.

His heart raced as Jesus drew nearer. Thoughts of, "What should I say to Him?" and "What should I do when He gets here?" raced through his mind.

Peter could not see everything that was happening, but there must have been a person healed with every step that Jesus took, for over and over he could hear a litany of emotional voices declare, "Oh thank you! Thank you so much Lord! Praise God; I've been healed!" and "Yes Jesus, I believe in You!" He knew not exactly what Jesus had healed them of, but that the Lord must have freed many from pain and anguish.

When Jesus was but a short distance away, Peter saw Him take a little child from his mother's arms. The small spindly legs dangled helplessly from the child as Jesus held him close. The Lord put His hand upon the child's head, said a few words, and handed the child back to his mother. Then Jesus motioned toward the ground.

With a look of utter amazement, the mother placed the child upon the ground as all who were nearby saw him stand for the very first time in his life. The child took his first wobbly step. His mother fell to the feet of Jesus while holding her child near with one arm and wrapping the other around His ankles. She thanked Him over and over again for healing her son.

Jesus simply placed His hand comfortingly upon the woman's head. Then, He resumed His walk down the hillside.

Faster and faster did Peter's heart beat with each step that the Lord took in his direction. Peter had never dared dream of such an experience as this. Every movement of Jesus was a holy experience. Everything Jesus touched was marvelously blessed in some way. Every glance that the Lord made seem to profoundly touch someone.

When Jesus was nearly upon him, Peter's eyes met the Lord's for a brief moment, and Peter immediately dropped to his knees. There were a few other people who had fallen to their knees as Jesus passed them by, but the vast majority, though they were greatly taken in by Jesus, did not actually show any sign of reverence toward Him. But the crowd did not know what Peter did. Peter knew that he was in the presence of the Lord of lords and the King of kings. He knew he was before the Lord God Almighty!

Revealael had said that they could not be seen by the people they would visit, but somehow Peter was sure that did not apply to Jesus. If they were actually present here then surely Jesus would know it. At any rate, Peter knew he was in the presence of the Lord Jesus and he was going to respond accordingly.

Looking up from his kneeling position, Peter could see the Lord passing directly in front of him. To Peter's surprise, Jesus reached out and placed His hand upon his head. In that moment, a flood of peace and joy filled him. His body surged with such a vast flood of power that he nearly passed out. Falling toward the ground, his movement was abruptly halted by the angel's outstretched arm.

Peter was in ecstasy. He felt like every cell in his body had experienced the presence of Jesus. He could do nothing except say over and over, "Thank you, Jesus! Praise you Jesus!"

When he had ceased praying aloud, Revealael said, "You have been blessed greatly here this day in many ways that you do not yet understand. Remember, though, that the reality for a Christian is the day-to-day walk with Jesus in obedience to the will of God.

"There are many in the crowd here today who will only stay as long as they think they are being entertained. When the miracles of healing and of bread stop, they will find someone else to run after. Great will be the enthusiasm and cries of praise while He enters Jerusalem to set up what they believe will be a powerful earthly kingdom. When that does not happen, they will leave Him alone to suffer and die for their sins.

"Now, I will show you the saddest and greatest moment that has been, and that will ever be, in the history of mankind."

Traversing the mysteries of time, Peter and Revealael stepped out into a place that appeared little different than the darkness within time's clouds. It reminded him of when as a boy he had witnessed a total eclipse of the sun. But now, it was more than just darkness at the wrong time of day, there was a feeling of dread in the air. It seemed certain that something terrible was happening.

Then Peter turned and saw it—Jesus hanging on the cross! They were crucifying the Lord of Creation!

A sick feeling instantly came over him. It was a scene he had imagined in his mind many times while looking upon a crucifix. But this was different. Now he actually was seeing Jesus suffer.

Abandoned by men, He could still be heard praying for them. Peter's eyes filled with tears as he saw the Lord's great love for mankind being poured out. He who had given so much to ease the pain of others was now virtually alone in His moment of agony.

Christ's mother and John were there at the foot of the cross. A few other women were a short distance away lamenting His fate under the watchful eye of a centurion.

There was also a crowd that had gathered some distance away. Peter wondered if they were there to show their support for Jesus or if they were only curious as to what would become of Him.

Then Peter heard someone in the crowd call out, "Jesus, we believe you're the Son of God. Come down off that cross and we'll follow you!"

"They don't want Him. They only want a savior who will satisfy their desires, don't they?" Peter asked, turning to Revealael, and noticing the angel was so moved by the spectacle before him that tears were forming in his eyes.

Peter marveled for a moment that an angel could cry, and then realized that he must be seeing a physical response to a much deeper spiritual reaction. "Knowing the Lord so well must make it extremely hard for an angel to watch Him suffer and die," thought Peter sadly.

Revealael's appraisal of the sad situation was short but to the point. He said, "In all times, the crowd seeks a savior who will serve their wants, not one to serve."

Peter fell to his knees and began to pray. He prayed that he would live his life in a way never to forget the grace being poured out before him this day. And he prayed for the crowd and everyone in all in the world. He prayed that all would hear the true Good News, follow Jesus, and come to everlasting life.

Peter prayed as he had never prayed before. He had always seemed to be lacking for words when praying, but not now. As he looked up at Jesus suffering on the cross for the sins of the world, he found the words to pray. There was much to say, for his heart ached for the pain of Divine Love, spurned and pierced before him.

After some time, he heard a cry from the One before him, "My God, my God, why hast thou forsaken me?" Sadly, Peter knew that Jesus was enduring the pain of every man's sin. With his own heart breaking, knowing the great injustice transpiring before him, he sat motionless and marveled, trying to comprehend the magnitude of Jesus' love. Peter wondered how the Lord could love mankind so much that He would freely take on all this suffering.

Knowing what Peter was thinking, Revealael softly said, "The words that the Lord has just spoken express the great loneliness that the world's sin has brought Him. He has paid the price for all the sins that were, are, and are yet to be, but His words speak of more.

"Jesus' words hold faith and hope. They are the first words of the twenty-second Psalm. It is about Him. It begins by expressing the feeling of being forsaken, but reveals a truly great faith and hope in God. Jesus is proclaiming a great trust in God. This is to be a monumental example for mankind."

Abruptly Peter's attention was brought back to Jesus by the cry, "Father, into thy hands I commit my spirit!" and then, "It is finished."

With that, Jesus bowed His head and gave up His Spirit. The earth quaked while thunder roared from the lightning bolts that lit up the sky. Clouds churned overhead and turned a dark shade of purple, as if to symbolize the royal nature of the One whom had died. It was as though the whole earth itself testified to the God of Creation who had honored it by His presence.

It was then that Revealael said, "Take my hand and I will show you the meaning of this."

Before he knew what happened, Peter found himself within the Temple, standing before the curtain surrounding the Holy of Holies. The curtain was ripped wide open, from top to bottom, and the Ark of the Covenant could be seen clearly inside.

"I read in the Bible where the curtain in the temple is torn in two," said Peter, "but I have never understood its significance. What does this mean?"

Still holding Peter's hand, Revealael answered with an obvious look of excitement, "The wall that separated God from man has been breached. No longer must sin and death hold mankind in bondage. The Savior has bridged the impassable gulf. Jesus has redeemed mankind. Alleluia!"

CHAPTER 7

Hope Eternal

*E*ffortlessly, Revealael once again overcame the dark boundaries of space and time. Entering their destination, Peter immediately recognized where they were. Revealael had returned him to further observe the pit of the demons.

The demons were in a frenzy of wild abandon. Around, and around, and around they went in their dance of desolation, with their chanting blending one with one in a gruesome celebration. And Peter knew that such universal distraction must surely have come from something they perceived to be another tremendous victory.

"Behold, the apex of futility," proclaimed Revealael. "The utter despair you witness is exactly that which is testified to in a verse of the ancient *Psalm of the Angels* where it declares:
> Round they go in their dance of despair;
> their flames of agony rise into the air.
> As the fire of God's love purges sin,
> their fires do purge all hope within,
> leaving nothing but a drop of distraction."

Then, from that horde of horror below came a voice that screamed with a spine-tingling squeal, "The victory is ours, we have won. The fools are ours now and they will be ours forever."

"Dance! Dance! Think what this means to us. All that luscious fuel for our fires," cried another demon as his voice trailed off into a hideous laugh that soon was joined by the perverted laughter of the entire evil multitude.

Then, as if on cue, the entire congregation of demons fell into absolute silence. Soon Peter could see a much more gruesome being appear within their midst. He knew from his previous experience that it was Lucifer.

Lucifer's present appearance made the first time Peter saw him seem very tame indeed. With his body glowing hotter than the fires that engulfed it, Peter wondered if it was Lucifer who made the fires flame. Smoke billowed forth from his mouth, and his eyes bugged out and glared with a burning-bright redness that made Peter's skin crawl.

"Why is he more hideous than the other fallen angels?" asked Peter.

"Remember, Peter, that what you are seeing is the physical expression of a spiritual reality," replied Revealael. "What you see does not even begin to do justice to the total depravation before you. Lucifer was one of God's most glorious creations. His fall into total disobedience and darkness of spirit has a greater and more noticeable effect upon creation and himself than it does on those who do not fall such a great distance."

Revealael's explanation was interrupted by the scene before them. Lucifer began to speak in a fierce roar. Peter could see the other demons tremble as he cried out, "Fools! Idiots! Blind and stupid beings! Have you no idea of what you are doing? Do you not know what has just happened? We have been tricked. We have been deceived through a devious, holy plot.

"He died. He was in my domain and yet He escaped. You let Him escape. It is not fair. It was a dirty-rotten deception. He had no right to foil my plan. This is my domain. I rule here."

And with that, the demons were uncontrolled in their sickening adoration for the disgusting beast that ranted before them. Their frightening worship of Lucifer went on for some time, until with a wave of his hand their lord silenced them.

"My victory over Him had been so sweet," Lucifer continued in his boastful rage. "It was so simple to overcome His silly honesty and openness. Yet, I knew He was powerful. I did not think I could hold Him forever. But still, this is my kingdom and he cheated and tricked me into allowing, even inviting, Him to enter."

Waving his arms wildly, he continued, "And you, you still have no idea of what has happened, do you?

"You are no better than the simple-minded humans. So caught up in what you consider victory that you have not even noticed what has happened right behind your backs. Numskulls! Idiots! The enemy has entered our domain and escaped with many, many prisoners!

"You were so caught up in your so-called 'victory' that you never checked to see what the enemy was doing here. You never noticed that He was preaching His filthy message of salvation to the captives. All you ever think about is easing your pain, your miserable, precious pain. Your distraction is always in the way of our victory. Well, I am sick of it. Sick!

"You have a job to do, and you know exactly what that is. You have a lower calling and it will be performed, or else you will all find that the great agony of your pain has only just begun to be revealed. I am your lord and king and you shall accomplish my will or know the consequences of failure!"

And falling down before Lucifer, they all worshiped him, pledging their allegiance and obedience to him in a chorus of unending words that at once sent a nauseating chill down Peter's spine.

Peter, turning to Revealael, was pleasantly surprised to see the angel's aurora starting to become visible. As it appeared to engulf everything in view, the aurora brought with it a sense of peace and joy to Peter that immediately turned his thoughts away from the evil ones and brought them to bear upon God and His greatness.

Feelings of peace, joy, comfort, and love flooded Peter's senses until he desired nothing else but to feel and look into the aurora. He felt closer and closer to God with each moment that he explored its glorious realm. To him it seemed as though God was dwelling within its wondrous beauty. Although, maybe it was just that the waves of light somehow proclaimed the glory of God that powerfully.

In any sense, the waves of energy from the aurora stretched out like gigantic walls of flowing multi-colored light. Though they looked as they did when Revealael first showed him the other Aurora Angels, he was now much closer and could feel his body being more acutely bombarded and immersed in each wonderful wave.

The aurora's beauty was beyond comprehension. With every dazzling color imaginable proceeding forth from Revealael in tantalizing waves that smoothly and effortlessly blended each changing hue into the next, Peter was sure that he was experiencing a perfect stimulation of the visual senses. It was a sight beyond compare.

Totally enraptured by the aurora, he became more confident the longer he had meditated upon it that it was a reflection of something much more than Revealael that he was seeing. In his inner being Peter somehow knew that this was no simple created power that he had been allowed to explore. Somehow this directly proclaimed the Divine.

Soon, from within the aurora, Peter's suspicions were proven true, as a dazzling light, brighter than the sun, appeared. Looking even more intently, Peter could see the light to be One like a man, dressed all in white.

The Man spoke and, though he heard not a word, somehow Peter could see the Word come forth from His mouth. The Word traveled for but a short distance, and then with a roar there poured forth from nowhere a seemingly endless supply of matter that in just a few moments formed stars and galaxies and planets in an otherwise empty domain.

Peter was totally awestruck by what he was seeing, but soon it was gone. While searching for what only moments before had been so clearly obvious, suddenly a new vision appeared to him.

In this new vision he saw the same One who previously spoke. His Word traveled down and struck the earth where its impact caused water to pour forth from a rock in the middle of the dessert. There was a multitude of people nearby that gathered around, giving God praise and thanks for the rock. Abruptly, the vision ceased.

Peter looked elsewhere in the aurora and again saw a vision of the Mighty One. This time the Word that came forth from Him struck the earth as a bolt of lightening. It destroyed an altar, stones around the altar, and even the water therein.

Those who were gathered there were shouting, "The Lord is the Almighty God!" And, as quickly as it had appeared, that vision was gone.

Peter looked, and in another part of the aurora he saw One who was dead hanging upon a cross and immediately recognized Him as Jesus. He could see Christ being taken off the cross and placed in a tomb, but before Peter could begin to feel sad, there was a blinding flash of light and death was turned into life!

He who was dead was now alive, dazzling brighter than the sun in His glory. Then, the Lord Jesus could be seen rising from the earth with an immense multitude singing His praises.

No sooner had the Lord vanished from sight into the heavens than Peter could see a snow-white Dove fly down to the earth. In a splash of fire, the Dove descended upon a group who was gathered in the upper room of a building and they began to enthusiastically praise God. Their praise was so intense that a large number of people gathered to see what had agitated these people.

Shortly thereafter, a large and burly man stood up and began to preach of the Messiah to those who had gathered. Peter was amazed at the ability of the large man to captivate the crowd with his message. Peter soon realized that the man was his namesake, Saint Peter, and that he was viewing the Day of Pentecost.

There were thousands of people gathered there. The young; the old; whether men, women or children; they all came forward to Saint Peter and the other Apostles to proclaim their faith in Jesus.

Peter thought, "Surely God is glorified this day." And with that, the visions disappeared from the aurora.

Peter felt as though his heart had been ripped from him. Hoping to continue this strange communion within the aurora, he searched the curtains of light for more, but even the aurora was fading. Soon the aurora itself disappeared.

Then, Revealael asked, "Now do you understand the meaning?"

"Understand what?" a bewildered Peter answered.

"From glory to glory," shot back the angel. "I know that you have often wondered what that meant. Now you have observed it. One glory leads to another and all glorify God.

"The radiance that you saw coming forth from me, the aurora, is not mine to lay claim to or possess, it is the glory of God shinning forth from within me. The visions that you saw within the glory are all part of God's glory, albeit a very small part.

"Even man's actions can give glory to God. When God is glorified, His glory shines out upon the one who glorified Him. That person is blessed from glory to glory. Great and amazing things begin to happen. Like a wildfire it spreads blessings everywhere. Such a simple concept and yet so hard to understand for men who are full of sin and pride."

"Looking at the glory of God, I didn't want to stop," confessed Peter. "I felt like my heart was being ripped out when the visions ended. I think I could have gazed into your aurora forever."

"I know," replied Revealael, "and that is why I have had to conceal it from you. You would not have wanted to leave the presence of God's glory. It is no fault on your part. If you would have been able to see the reality of glory at all times, I could not have shown you all that you needed to see. Unfortunately, all that must be known is not glorious.

"It is because of God's glory shinning forth from me that the demons cannot see me. Through their choice they are forever deprived of the glory of God and cannot see nor understand it. But through the holy angels' choice, they are forever engulfed in the glory of God and at all times see Him who is glorious beyond all description.

"I truly wish that you could fully see the glory of God. For His glory extends far beyond what you can now comprehend. Only those who have reached the end of their earthly life in God's grace and have been transformed by the Lord Jesus into perfect holiness may see the fullness of the glory of God."

"I am thankful to have seen what I have," said Peter. "Although, it amazes me why you have revealed these things to me."

"As I said before," answered the angel, "it is God's will. Listen to Him. Proclaim the glory of God to all who will listen. To proclaim God's glory is to experience it. To be able to go anywhere and do anything, yet constantly be engulfed in the glory of God is beyond all words and description. Your hope is the reality that is mine—to eternally behold God.

"There is much to rejoice over. Jesus has conquered sin and death. Alleluia! Hope Eternal has arisen. For to all who follow Jesus is this hope given. All who believe and follow to the end will also reign victoriously forever in the glory of God. This is the 'Hope Eternal.'

"Now we must go. We have much more to see, since the real struggle has only just begun. The demons will not relent in their pursuit of souls. They have nothing else to do but wallow in their pain and acquire any drop of distraction that they can find through human agony and destruction."

And before Peter could utter a word, the dark clouds rolled in.

CHAPTER 8

The Battle of Will

Black clouds churned everywhere until Revealael led Peter through the portal into a world shimmering in multi-colored light. Peter soon recognized that he was once again seeing the glorious light radiating from the other aurora angels. There was simply nothing else like it. "How magnificently," he thought, "does their light fill the darkness and dispel the fear of evil."

When he saw them before their beauty had captivated him, but now, he couldn't stop searching for a fuller revelation of the glory of God. It was amazing how a little understanding had changed his perspective.

Then he noticed Revealael staring at him, waiting for some response and so he simply asked, "Why are we here again?"

"I have much more of the demon's ways to reveal to you and I wanted you to see the manifestation of the glory of God again before we descend into their pit," answered Revealael.

"Isn't it enough to know that mankind has a fallen nature that is prone to sin and that the demons diligently work to encourage people to sin?" questioned Peter.

"No," answered Revealael. "Even knowing that, people continually fall into the traps that the demons set for them. Because of pride, people have a hard time accepting the fact that the demons are of greater intelligence, craftier, and more powerful than they. When some do accept the reality of demons, they usually attribute them with human characteristics and powers. One envisions creatures who are nothing but a joke and hence no real threat. And so one even sees commonplace things in your world named after the devils as though they were of no significance.

"This harmless understanding is exactly what the demons want mankind to believe, that is, if they cannot get you to discount them all together. They, of course, prefer people to believe that the fall of disobedient angels, the creation, and the fall of man are just fables that have been made up to express certain pious generalities about mankind. The demons know that before one can fight an enemy one must first believe the enemy exists, and so they remain hidden. To fight an enemy effectively one must respect their power, and so, if they are believed in at all, they prefer to be thought of as fools.

"Many people will not believe anything that they can not obviously perceive, so they remain ripe for the demons to harvest in their lies and craftiness. Fearing to step out in faith, many remain in what they think is a safe reality, but they are constantly within the grasp of the evil ones. They are far from seeing the truth that is found only through God's grace."

"But how can one be sure he is in the truth?" asked Peter.

"Only by walking in the Word of the Lord can one be sure," answered the angel. "Only by trusting in God and His ways can a man be sure he is living in truth. To the one who believes and trusts in Him, God will reveal the truth. God desires faith to be alive in all men, just as he did in Abraham.

"Most people only want to believe in what they see and understand. But understanding is not faith. Faith is believing in and acting upon what one cannot see or understand. Believing the obvious is simply knowledge. Knowledge is good if it brings one to God.

"But isn't faith a gift?" questioned Peter while shrugging his shoulders. "If faith is a gift, then people say why worry about it. I either have it or I don't. I've heard that a lot."

"True, faith is a gift," replied the angel, "But that must be explained. Some try to excuse a lack of faith by saying, 'Faith is a gift of God, so if one has it or not is God's responsibility.' This is not what God has revealed to be the reality.

"God is, of course, the provider of all good things. Faith is a gift, but it comes about in an indirect way, not a direct way. God provides a universe full of good things; God provides man with a free will; and then God draws the heart towards trusting in Him. One uses that which has been given to decide for or against believing in God. God's grace plus a person's decision to step out and actually follow His will equals faith in God.

"Man's perspective should be in thankfulness to God. All have been gifted and now it is up to each person, through what has been given, to respond to God in faith.

"Now we will look at the opposite of faith. The demons know that there is an Almighty God, but they have no faith whatsoever, nor can they. Because of the glorious way in which they were created, one act of disobedience was an eternal choice, which brought about an eternal separation from God. Their only relief, if one could call it that, is through the distraction that comes from reveling in human misery.

"The world must come to understand where the real battle is being fought. One must understand who the enemies are if one will defeat them. The real battle is not against flesh and blood, but is against the principalities and powers, the rulers of this world of darkness, the demons. This is no small warfare that is happening in our midst. It is a mighty battle."

While motioning downward into the dark, red glow below them, Revealael took Peter by the hand and began leading him into the demons' pit. Down and down they went into that dwelling place of anguish.

In this closer examination, he observed that it was like a huge honeycomb with many levels all having a multitude of rooms. Through all they traversed there seemed to be one overwhelming and consistent factor—the projections of doom, despair, and pain that reached out from every direction.

"Do they know that we are here?" asked Peter. "It seems like they are trying to ensnare me with their evil."

"No," replied the angel, "they do not know we are here. They are at all times trying to entrap someone; that is what you sense."

Entering a chamber where two of the demons were having a heated discussion, they stopped and Revealael explained, "These are two principalities, Belamar and Kolar. They are two of Lucifer's primary lieutenants, and they are formulating their battle plan in response to Christ's Resurrection."

"No! I tell you we do not want to attack them head on," Kolar screamed as he flung his arms wildly into the air. "If there is anything we should know, it is the power of deception. We must come at them from their backside, attacking them subtly while their minds are preoccupied."

"Maybe so," countered Belamar, "but we have had successes with the frontal attack too, right from the beginning. Lord Lucifer overcame Eve with a direct assault. Look at the outcome."

"Yes, look at it!" shouted Kolar. "Our kingdom is in shambles. The Enemy has run off with our possessions and lord Lucifer is in a state like I have never seen him before. You must remember that much has changed since he fooled that first woman in the garden. I know it is hard to believe, but I have heard that some of the humans have actually begun to think. And now, they have a tendency to mistrust us!"

"You are right," admitted Belamar, "we must constantly be willing to change our direction of attack if we are to surprise and fool them. It is just that I don't think we should totally disregard the idea of using a direct assault. I'm sure it can sometimes still work."

"Very well," replied Kolar switching his mood and tone of voice to one that was more amiable, "we will be open and flexible to a variety of strategies."

"Actually, what our lord Lucifer accomplished with Eve centered around some deception mixed in with the truth," mused Belamar. "That is still a good plan. It has worked well for us to take the Enemy's Word and twist it around so that our will can be accomplished.

"The Enemy commanded the man, 'You may freely eat of every tree of the garden; but of the tree of the knowledge of good and evil you shall not eat, for in the day that you eat of it you shall die.' The woman did not listen carefully to the Enemy's Word and was confused into thinking that He also said, '...neither shall you touch it, lest you die.'

"Our lord Lucifer taught us much in this first encounter with the humans. It is a splendid example to follow.

"First, he confused the woman's understanding of the Enemy's Word. That encouraged her to believe that the Enemy's exact Word was unimportant and was therefore eligible for critical interpretation.

"Secondly, through her newfound justification to interpret the Enemy's Word, he convinced her to dwell in the close proximity to disobedience, and she touched and held the forbidden fruit. After seeing that she did not die upon touching the fruit, it was a simple matter convincing her to go one step further and eat it."

"You're right about that," agreed Kolar. "They usually do fall for that one. It is easy to get them to think that the Enemy is just like them and thinks and speaks in haphazard fashion. Little do they know how important is every single word to Him. We must continue to use that strategy, it has worked very well."

"All the better for us," gloated Belamar, as he belched out a sickening laugh. "If we can't get them to ignore the Enemy's Word then we'll convince them into rationalizing it into what they want it to mean. We'll convince them that the Enemy's Word needs to be updated for their enlightened age."

"Yes," chimed in Kolar, enthusiastically, with a sadistic grin, "and we'll even help them update it!

"The most important thing is to gain ground with them, no matter how small the victory. Anytime we can draw them even a little farther from the Enemy we have won a great victory. If we remain patient, all the little victories will win us the final triumph. Our perseverance is much greater than that of the silly humans. The Enemy's plan will surely be defeated."

"Anything that we can do to get their minds off of the Enemy is a victory," agreed Belamar. "We need to keep our perspective. We don't have to get them to bow down and worship us; all we have to do is get them to keep their thoughts centered on themselves or material possessions and we will win. Anything to keep them from worshiping and obeying the Enemy will give us the victory."

"You are quite correct in your understanding of the problem," interjected Kolar. "They often start out very seriously in following the Enemy, but soon become lax. We don't want to fall into the habit of writing off those who are hot in their pursuit of the Enemy. We must constantly remind our troops not to give up when they cannot at first get the humans to reject Him. If we persevere we will wear them down. We will gradually drag them down and slowly but surely achieve our ultimate victory.

"As you well know, the general rule for first attacking those seriously committed humans is to get them to think that they do not need to spend so much time talking and praying to the Enemy. Remember, if they don't listen to Him they will not follow Him. Instead, they will follow their idea of who the Enemy is and what He wants of them; that will always be wrong. They will drift towards their selfish will and the ways of the world."

"I have found it quite effective in such cases to encourage the humans to get involved in some organization or project that will occupy their time," said Belamar. "Even if it were what the humans would consider a good cause. If it takes them away from time spent seeking and directly serving the Enemy then it is a victory for us.

"We have to be careful, of course, because there are some of their organizations, which glorify the Enemy. They are few, but we must be mindful of them. Although, this is not too much of a problem. The foolish humans can be easily led into thinking that all that is important is for them to do good and not that they do good in the service of the Enemy.

"Soon they will be convinced that the only thing important is to do good deeds. Thinking it is superfluous to speak of sin, redemption, and salvation, we will have them right where we want them. They will go so far as to call themselves missionaries but never preach His Gospel. They will spread a religion, alright, but not the one the Enemy has commissioned them to spread. They will witness to a gospel of good-works whereby man works to save himself, and we will have won."

"It is as I have said many times," pronounced Kolar, "All we need do is turn them from the Enemy and they will be ours. They think they are so wise and strong. Ha! Little do they know that they either serve Him or us. They are never their own masters.

"All we have to do is distract them enough and they will become lukewarm in their desire to follow the Enemy. The Enemy will not tolerate their being lukewarm and they will soon be ours; it's that simple.

"I believe that our troops will find much of this work done for them by the foolish humans if they but have the patience to wait for it to be accomplished. The great pride of the humans and their unending habit of rationalizing everything out to fit their desire will often do the bulk of the work.

"The humans, on their own, will often very nicely serve themselves, all the while saying they trust and believe in the Enemy. He tells them that they must be either for or against Him, but still all they do is give Him lip service and then do their own thing.

"The Enemy tells them that they must do more than call out 'Lord, Lord,' but that is what their natural tendency would have them do. If we can get them to follow their natural desires, we will do very well indeed."

"Yes," agreed Belamar enthusiastically. "If we can keep their attention upon themselves and the world around them we will have won the greater part of the battle. The Enemy has formed within them a natural need to seek a higher meaning and purpose in life. He gave them this desire in order to lead them back to Himself, but we can most certainly use it to our advantage.

"All we have to do is convince them that what they can see and touch is of more importance than what cannot be seen, and they will be worshiping each other, animals, and the earth itself. Oh, they will not recognize it as worship when they make those things occupy the center of their lives, but that is exactly what it will be."

"Enough talk then," retorted Kolar. "Let us assemble the troops and begin our new assault. I can hardly wait." And in a moment, he and Belamar vanished into the darkness.

"That was enlightening," confessed Peter. "I never realized that the evil ones were so involved in the world."

"Then you have just begun to understand the magnitude of the problem," replied Revealael, "but there is much more to know."

AURORA ANGELS

CHAPTER 9

True Wisdom

"Monsieur Newforte, I tell you, since these ideas have been introduced to the people I have seen the souls of more men ruined than in all the rest of my life," pleaded the elderly man in the long black robe. "They have traded their inheritance for a swine's meal."

Normally a very mild-mannered man, the bishop was noticeably upset by his guest. His face turned a pale red that contrasted acutely with his snow-white hair.

"Come, come, Bishop," Newforte boomed back as he strutted his tall frame across the room, "the people have simply been awakened to their potential to think and reason. This is the eighteenth century, my good man, not the eighth. It is a great age, an enlightened era. The people know how to think. They can judge for themselves what is right and what is wrong."

"I couldn't possibly disagree with you more," countered Bishop LaRock. Pointing toward North America on a map of the world that hung on the wall, he continued, "One could only rely on one's conscience to guide him after it has been properly formed. To expect otherwise would be much like sending a young child out to sea as captain of a ship heading for America. The child may very well indeed wish to be a good ship's captain and want very much to reach America, but his good intentions would in no way ensure that he would reach his destination. Good will is no substitute for good training and preparation.

"To you, I maintain that what we have seen happening around us is not something new. It is rather something that is very, very old—rejection of God's ways. You may call it 'enlightenment,' but I call it rejecting God and following darkness. It is nothing but sin.

"The ideas we see being spread fit unmistakably into what is called the Reciprocal Principle of Morality. I'm sure you've heard of it. It states: 'The degree to which a man accepts a man-made morality is directly proportional to the degree which God's revelation of morality is rejected.'

"The greater a man's disdain for God we find the greater will be his desire to place some thing or idea at the center of his life. It is simply a false god of his choosing. The only relatively new thing we have happening at this time in history is the widespread attempt of men to rationalize their sin."

After absorbing the conversation he had been placed in the midst of for several minutes, Peter admiringly mused, "I sure wish we had Bishop LaRock back home, but that's not possible is it? We are in eighteenth century France, aren't we?"

"Yes," answered Revealael, "we are witnessing one of the greatest defenders of the faith to be found in France at the height of their so-called 'enlightenment.' As to finding Bishop LaRock in the twenty-first century...well, with God all things are possible."

Monsieur Newforte, who had been pacing the room in a small circle as the bishop spoke, now, after a moment of silence, abruptly resumed the conversation, "My dear Bishop, all we are trying to do is seek the truth. Surely you are not opposed to truth are you?"

"Of course not," answered the bishop. "I love the truth, because Jesus is the Truth, and the Way, and the Life. The Lord is Truth Incarnate."

"But, are there not other truths," interjected Newforte deviously while stroking the ends of his long, black mustache.

"What you are proposing is a so-called 'wisdom' of the world," explained the bishop. "It will never lead you to truth. Oh, it will uncover some aspects of truth, but it has not the power to find God, the Ultimate Truth.

"The Scriptures speak of a certain 'wisdom of this age' which is unable to see the Truth that comes from God. Truth can only be seen clearly through the wisdom that comes from the Almighty. It is a wisdom that the world cannot understand. The world sees it as foolishness.

"The Scriptures say, 'For the word of the cross is folly to those who are perishing, but to us who are being saved it is the power of God.' The true Christian finds meaning in the world only through Christ's cross, while the worldly person only finds Christ's cross a stumbling block that seems meaningless to him. The cross remains the same for both, only the eyes that view are different. It is a question of faith."

"Please now, Bishop LaRock, are you saying that I have not faith?" Placing his hands on his heart, Newforte continued, "I have been a Catholic all my life. I was baptized, confirmed and married in the Church. My grandfather, as I'm sure you know, gave to the Church the very land on which your cathedral stands. Surely you do not doubt my standing in the Church?"

"Why, Monsieur Newforte," continued the bishop. "I could not judge the condition of your soul. I would not try to do that. All I can do, in fact, have been ordained to do, is call attention to ways of thinking and actions that are contrary to the faith. And as sure as there is a heaven and a hell, there is also a definite body of belief that we call the deposit of faith that has been handed down to us through the ages directly from the Apostles themselves.

"As bishop, my foremost calling is to proclaim and preserve that deposit of faith that was handed on to me. I can strive to do no less, even if that means being unpopular with some people. It is the truth of the Gospel of Jesus that has the power to set men free from the bondage of sin and death. Removing anything from the Gospel hinders its power to save!

"When one begins diluting the Gospel one puts himself on very precarious ground. Unfortunately, it is such an easy thing to do. Wanting to please people is a very natural path to follow, but the Christian has a supernatural calling. The ordained teacher must look beyond what people want and set his sight onto what they need. The two are often quite different.

"Jesus knows what is needed to heal the heart of man. Being faithful to His Word ensures that mankind receives the proper medication. A sweetened gospel may be easier medicine to take, but after it has been modified it no longer has the strength required to heal the patient.

"It is hard to remain faithful when one is being ridiculed, but that is what all Christians are called to do. The great Saint Paul says, 'For I am not ashamed of the gospel of Christ for it is the power of God unto salvation to every one that believeth,' and I heartily agree with him. It may at times seem much easier to change the Gospel into something which the world will accept than to simply proclaim it, but proclaiming it as it was handed on to us is exactly what we are called to do."

"So, you really believe that a book that is eighteen hundred years old understands more about what the people need than the people themselves do?" Monsieur Newforte replied shaking his head in disbelief.

"Absolutely!" stated the bishop forcefully. "The people of this age understand well the things of the world, yet when it comes to the things of faith they are close to being totally ignorant. At best they are as infants. They need to be fed on the basic milk of the Gospel.

"Spiritually, most of the people have never grown. They are concerned only about their own needs and what they can acquire from the world. They do not understand and believe in anything except what they can see, and so they do not strive to do the will of the unseen Creator.

"Always learning, yet they are never able to come to a knowledge of the truth, because they ignore the Word of life that God has given them. God's Word was not given to only one time and place, but is meant for all people and all time as Saint Peter points out in his First Letter, 'For all flesh is as grass, and all the glory of man as the flower of grass. The grass withered, and the flower thereof falleth away: But the word of the Lord endureth for ever. And this is the word which by the gospel is preached unto you.' "

Flinging his arms into the air, Newforte snarled, "You want us to believe what we cannot understand and follow what we cannot see?"

"Most definitely, Monsieur, I do," returned the Bishop passionately. "But not for myself, as if it were something I could change. God demands it! The Almighty requires that everyone who comes unto Him must have faith in Him.

Man is saved through faith, not by understanding all things. Knowledge is good if it leads people to God, but it cannot save! Only through the sacrifice of the spotless Lamb, Jesus, can salvation be attained.

"Ah, and now we are back once again to that stumbling block of the cross. In human understanding, salvation comes through believing in a senseless act. The so-called 'wisdom' of the world rejects this. This is where faith comes into play. This is where it is necessary to step out in faith upon the waters, as Saint Peter did, although we are unable to understand how it is possible. We step out in faith and believe.

"Saint Paul in his Letter to the Hebrews tells us, 'Now faith is the substance of things hoped for, the evidence of things not seen.' Faith is trusting in the One we claim to follow. It is believing and following His Word, especially when we do not see or understand."

Unwilling to accept what he was hearing, Newforte shot back, "You speak convincingly, Bishop LaRock, but you must know that not all your associates speak in the manner that you do. For example, I personally know several priests and a bishop who do not believe in moral absolutes as you do. There are many who would say that the morality of what someone does can only be ascertained by the end result that it brings."

"The situation may well be as you say," admitted the bishop, "but what is right and wrong cannot be decided by a majority opinion. The Church has taught this from the beginning. God speaks clearly on the subject, and He is the same yesterday, today, and forever. Evil cannot be made into good by our wishing it or proclaiming it to be so.

"Now it is true that one's degree of guilt in performing an evil act depends on the seriousness of the act, the person's knowledge of the act's sinfulness, and their free desire to perform the act. Regardless, these considerations do not change evil into good. Doing evil is never good. God desires no one to do that which He calls evil.

"Opinion polls tell us nothing about truth, except that many in the Church have drifted far from its teachings. If one wants to find the truth they need only look to what the Church has consistently taught as far back as the time of the Apostles.

"There have been times when in some areas even the majority of priests and bishops have been in error, such as in the third century when the Arian heresy swept through the Church, or in the time of Henry VIII in England. In spite of those times when many people fell from the faith, the Holy Spirit preserved the Church, as Christ promised, and the teaching of the Apostles prevailed.

"There has always been a great temptation for those who teach and preach to buckle in to the desires of those they are called to minister to. We all can show a great resistance to face up to our sins. It is much easier to find excuses for them and rationalize them away. One who teaches must be rock solid in their faith or they will be swept away in the sea of popular opinion.

"It should be of no great surprise that the people are in great numbers rejecting the one, true faith and are professing a man-made religion. They seek to believe in that which will not challenge them to repent of the sins that they love. Saint Paul prophesied of this in his Second Letter to Timothy when he said, 'For the time will come when they will not endure sound doctrine; but after their own lusts shall they heap to themselves teachers, having itching ears; And they shall turn away their ears from the truth, and shall be turned unto fables.' That time is here!"

Looking thoughtfully, Peter said, "It sounds as though the problems the Church is experiencing in my time have their beginnings here in this enlightenment."

"Of course, it all began with the Original Sin, but in a real sense you are correct," agreed Revealael. "These ideas do not die easy. Although, you must realize that there is also much more going on in this room than two men with two contrasting sets of beliefs."

"There are?" said Peter looking about the room.

"I will show you," said the angel as he raised a hand.

Peter looked back toward the men in the room and found a scene quite different from what he had previously beheld. Standing behind Bishop LaRock was a being who appeared to be an angel. The angel was dressed in a long white robe and he glowed with a beautiful white light that radiated out from within his semi-transparent body. Since his one hand was upon the bishop's head while the other was lifted above him, the angel appeared to be praying over him.

Directly behind Monsieur Newforte stood two gruesome creatures with burnt-red flesh who Peter immediately recognized as demons. They appeared to be whispering something to Newforte from time to time as they continued an ongoing conversation with each other. All the while Newforte was as oblivious of the devils as they were of Peter and Revealael.

Peter's attention was drawn toward Monsieur Newforte and his gruesome companions as he began to hear the demons speak, and it was only then that he recognized them.

"You see, Primary," said Belamar, "have I not carried out your instructions well? The troops and I have begun a large movement of new thought that is on the verge of upsetting the entire social structure of the world. It is all working out exactly as you predicted."

"Yes," replied Kolar, "you have a good start, but do not let yourself be carried away from the great task that remains before us by this little piece of victory. Remember how foolish we looked at the time of the Enemy's great deception, when he tricked us into thinking He was dead. Lord Lucifer would not be pleased to have a repeat blunder of that magnitude. You know what that would mean, especially to you!"

"Primary, I assure you nothing like that will happen now," promised Belamar in a very consoling voice. "Your plan, great Primary, is flawless. I will ensure that it is carried out exactly according to your wishes. The humans will not know what has hit them, until it is too late."

"It had better be," warned Kolar, "or hell will see you pay!"

Peter cringed when he heard Kolar's warning. For a moment he pondered what must be the terrible depth and horror of this threat that he so often casually heard among humans. He wondered what had happened to now rank Kolar at a higher position in the kingdom of evil than Belamar, and so he asked his heavenly companion, "Revealael, what has happened that Kolar now has the title of Primary?"

"Belamar is about to unwittingly answer that question for you," answered the angel.

"Truly Primary," continued Belamar, "your plan is a masterpiece. It is undoubtedly the greatest attack ever formulated. The one possible exception, of course, being your brilliant work in the Great Division. That was beyond compare, as it rightfully caused our lord Lucifer to elevate you to the most exalted position of Primary.

"Splitting the Enemy's followers up and dividing them into rival camps was pure brilliance. You have truly learned, with perfection, our lord Lucifer's ways of perverting the Enemy's Scriptures. The fools don't begin to realize how much in their pride they have helped build up the kingdom of darkness.

"Tearing each other apart, they have shredded the very thing the Enemy wanted most for them—unity in Him. Primary, your plan was of true brilliance. So much of their efforts are now being diverted toward battling each other, with their thoughts and words centered so intensely on the correctness of what they each believe and do, that they spend very little time actually working for the Enemy's Kingdom.

"And as a bonus, Primary, your Great Division has made it nearly impossible for them to counteract the marvelous plan of attack you have now formulated in their Enlightenment. The Enemy's Kingdom has been divided and cannot withstand our assault. I foresee our ultimate victory coming soon."

"Do not let yourself become too swollen with pride, Belamar," cautioned Kolar, "The Enemy is very cagey and can be expected to come up with surprises of His own. He has fooled us before and I am sure He will try to do so again. But, it is good that in the meantime we have won over many humans into the kingdom of darkness. Those many points of distraction have been most welcome.

"As I have told you many times, and as you can now obviously see, Belamar, the indirect attack is much more effective. The beauty of our present position in the battle is that the stupid humans do not even begin to realize that it is we who are the real architects and builders in their world. We have led them to the point where they are hard at work for us while at the same time thinking they are finally their own masters. Ha! The ignorant fools, they think they are worthy to be masters of the universe, but they will only be our playthings and our fodder!"

"Your wisdom is indeed grand, O Great Primary," whined Belamar.

"Yes, and you have done well to follow my instructions," replied Kolar proudly. "If you continue to serve me well, I will allow you near me to be distracted by the spoils in our ultimate victory. Together with our lord Lucifer, we will devour the ignorant humans forever!

"For now though, there is much work to be done. You can easily assign a lower worker to Newforte at this time, he is firmly ours and needs only to be gently guided to perform our will.

"Our immediate goal is to reinforce into the minds of the humans the thought that there are no moral certainties. We must work towards convincing them that there are no objective truths; everything is relative to how one thinks or feels. If we can convince them that the end result justifies any means used to get there, then we can get even the best of them to do anything.

"Bishop LaRock is a totally different story, but we should in no way think that his fate need be the same as Newforte's. LaRock, and those like him, who remain in the Enemy's Kingdom, can still be of service to us. Just getting him to falter from his faith in small ways, occasionally, can serve us. Although, I think we have a greater potential in even one so firmly entrenched in the Enemy's camp as he.

"LaRock has been one of the few faithful servants in a high position that the Enemy has. He speaks the Enemy's message and he knows it. How easy it would be to fill his head with thoughts of self-righteousness and pride."

"Yes, pride is the foothold," piped in Belamar, as he beamed with a devious grin. "We will use pride to make him just a little less effective in proclaiming the Enemy's position. I will put one of my most capable workers on him and oversee the project myself."

"Very well then," agreed Kolar, "let us not be like the humans and waste the moment!"

With that, Peter suddenly found himself alone with Revealael in the midst of the dark swirling clouds.

"Are things as bleak for the Kingdom of God as they say?" asked Peter.

"Only if Christ's followers sit by idly," answered the angel. "The Lord has called them to work for His Kingdom, and that they must do. God desires to work through His children, for there is still much to be done in building His Kingdom. Know for sure, though, that God will be there to strengthen and guide His followers every step of the way.

"The evil ones are very cleaver, cunning, and convinced that they can ultimately win the battle. Indeed, as I told you before, this is a great battle that they and we are engaged in. But do not lose heart, for greater is He who is within you than he who is in the world. The demons do not realize the awesome power of God. All things are possible with the Almighty.

"God's children must look to their Savior for strength. Keeping faithful eyes fixed firmly on Jesus will bring victory to those who are called by His Name.

"Be assured, in the end, Christ will reign victoriously."

CHAPTER 10

The Unchaining

With clouds already beginning to form around them, Peter barely had time to collect his thoughts enough to ask, "Revealael, did I just observed all that was going on in that room?"

"No," the angel answered without hesitation. "Those were the only evil beings, but there were other angels present, coming and going as need arose. If I were to show you all that was happening in many situations on the earth, you would only grow more confused.

"The Almighty works in many mysterious and wonderful ways. But don't be alarmed that you do not understand everything. As for the demons, they do not even begin to understand all that God is doing, much less why He does what He does. They have nowhere near the amount of control over situations that they think they do.

"The holy angels understand nearly all that God is doing in the world, but even some things are beyond our present knowledge. It is enough for us to simply do the will of God and to behold His Face.

"Listen and I will tell you a great mystery. Even though we constantly behold the Almighty, the mind of God is so vast that it will take us an eternity to totally experience Him. The glory of God is like a never-ending river that continuously flows through us. It floods us with knowledge, wisdom, and refreshing baths of comfort, peace, and joy."

"That sounds so wonderful!" exclaimed Peter longingly. "Please tell me more about God."

"It is good that you want to understand Him better. The Almighty wishes you to one day know Him fully. But at this present time He desires you to understand more fully the workings of your foe and the great battle you are engaged in," replied the angel. "There is still more that you must see."

Quickly, the churning clouds engulfed them and their journey resumed. Peter wondered if their travel through them was essential or if the clouds were only a visual effect for his benefit.

Before he could pursue that thought, the portal appeared and they stepped into a destination that Peter immediately recognized.

Down they went through the chambers of hell. As they passed through one, and then the other, Peter witnessed a varied assortment of gruesome scenes and situations. From the moaning and cries of excruciating agony and pain, to demons at their dance of distraction, one thing throughout was common—the utter horror of creatures lost in the darkness of sin.

Shortly, they entered a vast, smoke-filled chamber. Around the room were a number of bubbling sulfur pits where, seemingly at their own discretion, flames of fire shot up from the chamber's floor.

In the center of the room was a long table, surrounded by ten small chairs and one large throne. Seated in each chair was a demon, with the throne occupied by Lucifer.

It was then that a demon, whom he had not noticed standing behind Lucifer, shouted out, "Bow down and worship your lord god!"

And with that cry, the assembly, all as one, rose from their seats; fell prostate before the one on the throne; and loudly proclaimed, "Hail lord Lucifer! Hail lord Lucifer!"

"Rise!" demanded Lucifer. "I am well worthy of your praise and admiration, but I have called you here for other matters.

"We have much work to do. With so little time, let us not waste the opportunity. Do not fear. I have not called this meeting of the principalities to chastise you, but rather simply to inspire you to continue onward with your delicious task.

"In fact, I have never felt so sure of our cause. I am confident my kingdom will soon be overflowing with luscious morsels of distraction. Soon more humans than we ever dreamed possible will be ours.

"Yes, comrades, things are beginning to fall into place. All the hard work and effort we have put forth into the building the kingdom is finally paying off. I can feel it in the very power ebbing forth from my being.

"I am amused to report to you that our official studies have shown our recent project, commonly known as the 'enlightenment,' was a huge success. We have indeed acquired many of the humans through its efforts, as I am sure you have all experienced. I would now remind you, though, the success of that project in claiming the miserable humans will be as nothing compared to the value of your efforts in using their 'enlightenment' as a building stone to new and even more prosperous efforts.

"Indeed, the Enlightenment firmly brought them into the age of Rationalism, and they look for a scientific reason for everything, otherwise they will not believe. No one plan of attack that we have ever formulated has been anywhere near as effective in combating that silly idea of 'faith' which the Enemy promotes.

"At this time, we must move onward. We must continue to build within the gullible humans the belief that everything old is bad and that only new things are good. We shall help them acquire modern things, as this will encourage them to also be more open to accept modern ideas. What is modern is therefore good. They will have modern tools, modern toys and modern ideas.

"We will help them build a modern society based on anything and everything material. Then soon they will have modern thinking, and, if we work hard, even a Modern Church.

"If we can get them to firmly establish Modernism into the Church we will turn the very camp of the Enemy into a powerless social club. Imagine the beauty of a church that is more concerned about the material than it is the spiritual. We will slip them down the slope of Modernism right where we want them—with us. They will all be our delicious distraction forever and ever."

Kolar spoke up and cautiously addressed Lucifer, "Most worthy master, lord of all the earth, how wise, indeed, has been your plan and guidance for our victory over the Enemy. We, your lowly servants, have followed your directions diligently, and you may be sure that we will continue to do so.

"Show us your plan, O lord, and we will carry it out to fulfillment. We are utterly amazed at your great genius in introducing the Enlightenment to the foolish humans; they snatched it up so fast that most can't even remember how or what they previously thought.

"Just as you foretold, after being introduced to the Age of Reason, they soon turned it into their Age of Rationalization and began looking for a provable and scientific explanation for everything. Of course, the pathetic creatures could not have done it without us, but they never suspected our involvement at all. They are so ignorant.

"Again, as you said, it was a simple matter to turn their attention to matters of morality. Humanism they call it. We call it a great day!

"I must confess, O great one, your wisdom surpassed mine greatly in seeing how they would even carry their rationalism to the point where they would formulate their social and moral codes through rational thinking alone.

"With our help, they have turned their social and moral standards upside down by accepting only those premises that could be demonstrated scientifically, or so they thought. It must have greatly irritated the Enemy for them to have rejected in such a short span of time the pronouncements that it had taken Him centuries to reveal.

"The vast throng accepts only what they can understand, and through your wise guidance, they have been successfully influenced by our troops to totally reject objective thinking. They have been brought to the point where they do not accept anything as absolute. To them, everything is subject to circumstances. I must admit, lord Lucifer, that sometimes, even after working among them for all these centuries, they amaze even me in their degree of stupidity.

"All we have to do now is gently build an excuse in their minds and we can convince them that any action is acceptable. If we cannot convince them that an action is subjectively correct, then we can show them some final goal that is acceptable to their perverted moral code, and they will agree to the otherwise unacceptable action because the end result will be acceptable. What morons these humans are; but they do make for good distraction.

"Lord Lucifer, since we have these humans firmly entrenched in modern thinking, where do we go from here? I know that you have more in store for them than this. Show us your plan. We will gladly carry it to completion."

"You have spoken well, my Primary," answered Lucifer while rising. "Recently, I feel a surge of strength as I ponder our plan of attack and imminent total victory. I feel that all our hard work is finally paying off. Everything is coming together for us and it will only be a matter of time before we totally defeat the Enemy.

"There is much yet that has to be done but together we can accomplish our task if we work diligently. I have a plan that will gain us access into every human heart. It is built firmly upon the Modernism that we have worked so hard to establish within their thinking. I call my plan the Sexual Revolution.

"Oh, I know that we have over and over again caused the fall of these humans through their sexual weaknesses, but what I propose now is a new concerted effort. My plan will not just make a few fall, but will change their social and moral perspective concerning sex in such a way that most of them will come to us. In the past, as soon as we made progress with an individual's sexual attitudes and actions, their society and religion would rise up against our progress and stifle its movement through their culture. Now, with this Enlightenment which we have brought to them, the Sexual Revolution will be unstoppable.

"Sex is a powerful force in the lives of the weak humans. The Enemy fashioned them in this way so that they would have offspring and subdue the earth. If we can mold their sexual morality into our liking, we will have them. There is a tremendous natural force involved here.

"As you well know, the Enemy is very touchy about these humans straying from His laws concerning sex. He thinks that because He made them a certain way that they should act according to His wishes. And so, all this will truly be doubly delicious. We will have the dual distraction of infuriating the Enemy while we are pulling the silly humans down into a trap that they cannot get out of. It will be a glorious victory!

"What we need to do first, though, is lead the world into a great war."

"But, mighty lord Lucifer, we have caused many wars, and as you well know, they help the Enemy as much as us," interrupted Goolar, one of the lesser principalities.

"Yes," continued Lucifer, "war often kills those whom the Enemy has not prepared for death, but also causes many of them to think of their mortality and listen to Him. What I propose is a war unlike any other war. This one could change the very nature of the humans' families. It would be a war whose effects would go far beyond the insignificant millions who would die as a result of it. It would make the one that the humans call the World War seem puny."

"We are at a time between the First and Second World Wars aren't we?" Peter quickly asked Revealael, not wanting to miss anything that was said, and turned to see the angel nod his head in agreement.

Lucifer rambled on, "We have them so hooked on science and technology that I promise you the weapons of this war will be far more powerful than anything before seen on the face of the earth. This warfare will not be contained on the battlefield, but will reach to the very cities and homes of the humans as never before imagined. It will touch the lives of the women and children in a magnitude that will change the course of the world; it will truly be magnificent.

"The silly humans have always had their homes and families as a source of strength; we will change that. If we can break up their families we will have done much to win them into my kingdom. The men will be taken away in such great numbers for this war that the women will have to take their place in the shops and factories. In the homes as well as the workplace, the women will be forced to do the men's work. We will use this to plant in their women's minds that it is in men's work that happiness is to be found.

"With the seeds of Modernism well planted within them, it will be easy to keep the women working out of the home after the war. Seeing all the material benefits available to them, it will be a simple matter to get the foolish humans to use their Rationalism to justify both parents working out of the home. They will easily be convinced that two paychecks could buy more pretty things than one. Once money becomes the primary goal of both parents, it will take little effort to split up their family. With children, parents, and grandparents separated, they will lose the moral stability the family has traditionally given them, and our job will become much easier.

"When we have firmly established within the human's morality that it is a necessary and even higher calling for the woman to work outside the home, we can proceed in earnest with the heart of our sexual revolution. They will surely have the desire, and for the first time in their history they will have the means, to keep their families small and the mother in the workplace; we will ensure it. Bringing together planning, hard work and science we will make contraception a common word and practice in their homes.

The Unchaining

"I predict my bold plan for their sex will be the tool that will unleash the fullness of Modernism upon the world. Fitting perfectly into their new plans for a working home, they will use their rationalism to justify its use as an insurer of quality over quantity of life. They have set their hearts firmly upon money and what money can buy. Only the things which money can buy will be important to them. The most money per person, or more accurately, the least number of people for their money, will be their battle cry.

"Yes, I know you are thinking that there will be less new humans for us to work at acquiring, but I tell you I guarantee our percentage yield per thousand humans born will be greatly increased. Brothers, the distraction will indeed be terribly great, and I have not yet begun to tell you the far reaches of my ingenious plan.

"Once contraception is a common way of life, free-love will become a by-word of the age. Women, working as men, will demand the joy of sex without responsibility or burden, as is so common in the men, thanks to our glorious efforts. Sex will not be used as the Enemy intended, but will be thought of as only a means of pleasure. It will be completely removed from bringing new life into the world.

"Though by no means a totally new approach, the concerted angle and magnitude of attack is refreshingly bold. We will strike at the very heart of the world's social, political, and religious structures. Yes, now is a unique time with a unique opportunity for our kingdom. The power of this age surges within me bringing a new sense of direction and confidence. And remember, this is only the beginning.

"After the pleasure of sex has become an end in itself, we will work at bringing out what will be our most glorious victory of this age—abortion. Forever, this will be known as the Age of Abortion, thanks to our efforts.

"We will not only work to make it acceptable to a few selfish humans, but we will corrupt their social and governmental systems to the point where it will actually be made legal. Through our efforts I know we can turn a few hundred abortions a year into millions. Again, we will use their delusion with science to persuade them. You must work hard at this; it is of utmost importance for them to be convinced that the availability of abortion is a moral good.

"I know, it's hard to imagine that we could have such good rewards for our efforts as to win them over into thinking that abortion is good, but I tell you our studies have shown that in due time we can convince a majority of them of that position. Isn't it beautiful to think of souls so dead that they think it good to murder their children? I lust for it!

"As an added distraction, think of how infuriating their actions will be to the Enemy. It surely will greatly pain the Enemy to see how they treat His new life, tearing it apart in the womb.

"Their search for pleasure will have no bounds. Soon in great numbers will their men lust one for another and their women also will do acts with each other that will give us great distraction as they bring out the anger of the Enemy. Remember how He spewed forth His anger upon Sodom and Gomorrah. I can confidently tell you that what I am speaking of leading the world into will be much greater for distraction than were the deeds of those cities.

"Their widespread lust for the same gender is a great sign for us. It signals our final, triumphant victory. To the Enemy, these actions are of the worst sort, coming from those on the face of the earth with the most hardened hearts. They have total disdain for Him as they hold His natural order in contempt. And, it is not only those who do such things that infuriate Him, but also those who approve of their unnatural conduct. The Enemy clearly reveals His feelings on this matter in the first chapter of His Book called 'Romans.' He will be furious! But, their consciences are dead. Isn't that luscious? A dead conscience is truly a wondrous distraction to behold.

"This is a good example of why I have told you time and time again that it is good for us to know the Enemy's written Word. You will never learn to outsmart the Enemy until you have understood how He thinks. And furthermore, how can one twist His Word in the minds of His stupid followers unless one knows what He has said? I warn you, this is no small matter that I speak of!"

"But, what will the Enemy's Church do during this time of attack?" asked Kolar.

"A good question," resumed Lucifer. "We will cover the specifics more at a later time, but be assured that we will not let the Enemy's Church go about its business without our help. Above all, we will work at building up an awareness of His commands to be non-judgmental and tolerant of all people. Here again, it is imperative for us to know His Word that we may pervert it to accomplish our goals. Simply put; where the Enemy speaks of toleration of sinners we will infuse within his followers the belief that they must tolerate sin. We will confuse the Enemy's followers about judgment and toleration so completely that they will be most ineffective in stopping my plan of attack.

"Be aware, that my ingenious plan will not stop here. We can never be satisfied in half-victories, even when they so infuriate the Enemy as same-gender lust does. Our vision must always be on total victory. Everlasting death with its goal of eternal human fodder must constantly be on our minds.

"So then, looking beyond, we will lead them down the slippery slope of seeking 'quality life,' until they eagerly accept euthanasia—mercy killing. The Enemy says that there is value in human suffering, but this is not yet scientifically provable and the weak humans can be easily swayed to reject His theory and accept our rational approach of killing off those in pain.

"First it will be those near death who are in pain. Later, anyone who suffers, either physically or psychologically, will be given death. And the beauty of this, as with all things, is that once it is socially acceptable there will be subtle, although often forceful, pressure on those in pain to end their lives.

"With a minimal effort on our part, people in pain, especially the elderly, can be easily made to feel they are a burden to their families and society. They will feel guilty for being alive and will want to end their lives.

"Those close to them will, of course, want to tolerate their wishes and not impose their morality upon the suffering souls, no matter how weak their wish to be released from life really is. In the best cases the friends and family will share in the guilt, and we will have built guilt upon guilt which is truly a marvelous situation for our work.

"From there it will be quite easy for the simple-minded humans to accept what has always been an abhorrence to those among them with a living conscience—infanticide. At that point it will take very little effort on our part. After accepting the killing of their unborn on such a widespread scale they will easily fall into our way of thinking.

"After all, what difference would it make to them if a baby were killed minutes before birth or minutes after birth? I find such thinking quite illogical, and I think they will also. I have confidence that logic will prevail over what little conscience they have left. If we work hard, we can create a culture of death in their midst that will infiltrate every aspect of their society. Isn't that a wonderful thought for distraction?

"Victory is ours, brothers, if we but grab hold of it. I want to impress upon you again how strongly I feel that things are now coming our way. The hour is ours. The victory is ours. Ours is the death, forever and ever! Ours is the distraction without end!"

Depressed by Lucifer's words, Peter questioned, "All of what he said seems to have happened in my time, how can he be stopped?"

"I still have more to show you," answer Revealael. "Man must repent and turn to the Lord of Life or there will be much suffering.

"Lucifer is not as wise as he imagines himself to be. He does not have understanding to go with his knowledge of the Word of God. If he really knew the Word of God he would realize that the surge of power and accomplishment that he now experiences is not due to his ability coming of age, but comes from the fact that his chains have been loosened. This is the unchaining that was prophesied two millennium ago by the Revelation of Saint John.

"Lucifer has been allowed more freedom in the world, and the battle grows fiercer. He has been unchained because the end grows near!"

AURORA ANGELS

CHAPTER 11

The New Age

As before, with the secrets of time and space hidden in the darkness of swirling clouds, Peter and Revealael headed toward a new experience. Peter had not long to ponder all that had been happening for in just a few short moments they arrived at their destination.

The clouds receded, revealing a large, beautiful city that lay directly below the hill where they were standing. The dome of a huge building caught Peter's eye, and he immediately realized they were near a place he had often seen but had never visited. It was Saint Peter's Basilica. The Vatican lay below them.

No sooner had Peter realized where they were when he also realized that they were not alone. Directly in front of him appeared Lucifer's Primary, Kolar, and another demon.

Peter could hear Kolar say, "This is definitely as close as I want to get, Goolar. Though I have spent much time with most of them, when they get together like this it makes me revoltingly sick.

"I remember back at their Council of Ephesus when I headed the Observation Legion and entered their discussion chamber. I got so sick from all their disgusting talk and putrid praying that I couldn't get any decent distraction for over a month.

"Well anyway, that won't be my fate this time, Goolar. This time you will lead our forces here at their Second Vatican Council. You can decide for yourself how close to the Enemy's forces you want to get.

"I am sure you can handle this situation, which is why I chose you for the job. You served me very well in Germany during the war and I know you will do so now. There will be even more souls gained here."

"Tell me, most deserving Primary," asked Goolar, "why is it that you do not at all seem bothered by the Enemy's bishops coming together in such a large number as this. Aren't you concerned that they will be planning and scheming to upset our lord Lucifer's plan for his world? I mean, much of the time in the past we have worked hard to keep them from working too closely together, and here they are, all together as one, yet you do not seem to be the least upset!"

"Goolar, Goolar, open your eyes!" Kolar mocked his underling. "Haven't you noticed the power of our lord as of late? The hour has come for him to claim his kingdom. Struggle and connive as they will, these silly humans are no match for the kingdom of Lucifer!

"They think that they are strong when they are gathered like this. They think that together they can win the world for the Enemy. Ha! It is we who have the strength and the wisdom and the power to win the ultimate victory for the kingdom of our lord.

"For every plan of attack that they come up with we will devise two; no, four; no, a dozen, to thwart their plan. And since they have come together from throughout the world to formulate their plans, we will send back with each of them our dozen counter plans. Their gathering together will make it all the simpler for us to attack the whole world.

"The real beauty is that after all these years many of them still do not recognize who they are up against. In their hearts, most still do not believe that we exist. We will exploit their stupidity to the fullest, you can be assured."

"Ah," exclaimed Goolar, "I see! My troops will find ways to foul up every one of the goody-documents they will formulate. We will use their own, good intentions to attack them. Whatever they write we shall twist around in the minds of those who attempt to implement it so that the intention they desired is lost. It shall be just as our lord Lucifer taught us at his first encounter with the humans in the Garden of Eden."

"Yes, exactly," reassured Kolar, "you have received and understand your mission perfectly. They have prayed for the Spirit to come to them through the windows of their Church that they have thrown open. It will be up to us to ensure that much enters into their open arms.

"Let them make their changes, Goolar. Let it become change for the sake of change. The more changes in the Church, the better. For when their members see the changes coming to them over and over, they will hardly notice where the change comes from or what it does. They will be ripe and ready for any change we can inspire someone to make."

"Yes, Primary," continued Goolar, perfectly in step with his master, "we will work with their attitude of change to give them a change all right. It will be a change for the good of the kingdom of darkness. We will usher in an age of change; a new age of our kingdom has come."

"That is exactly what we need," proclaimed the Primary. "A New Age!"

With a wave of his hand, Revealael again brought the dark clouds upon them and in a few heartbeats they were at a place that Peter recognized well.

"We are at my home parish," Peter remarked as he looked around. "What could be happening here?"

"That is exactly the point of our being here," answered the angel. "Blessed Virgin is a very typical parish of this age. What will happen here will become an all too common happening in parishes throughout the world."

"Look! That's Father Strong," said Peter while pointing at a gray-haired priest standing in the rectory doorway. "He is the priest that baptized me as a baby. I don't really remember him, but I recognize him from the pictures that my mother has of him. I think he retired when I was very small.

"But, why are we here? My parents were quite fond of Father Strong. They always said that he was a good and holy priest, obedient to God and Church."

"Yes, you have been correctly informed," answered Revealael. "Father Strong has been a holy and faithful priest, but, against his wishes, he will soon be ordered to retire. It seems he has not kept up with the modern ways of operating a parish. To satisfy those in power, he will be replaced. This now is slightly before that time."

Peter could now see why Father Strong was standing in his doorway, as he was about to greet a visitor. A younger man was coming up the walk.

"Welcome," said Father Strong, somewhat unsure of whom he was greeting in the jeans, western shirt, and cowboy boots.

"How ya doing?" replied the visitor.

"Ah, yes, hello Father Small. It's good to see you again," continued Father Strong. "I had to look twice to be sure it was you. It has been such a long time since I was at Sacred Heart Parish, and you were only a boy then, but now a priest. Your mother must be very pleased. How is your mother? I heard she had been ill."

"She was better the last time I saw her," he answered. "You know her, tough as a boiled owl."

"I don't know about that. What I remember about your mother is her heart of gold, always ready to help someone in need," replied Father Strong, somewhat taken aback by Father Small's crude remark.

"You look quite well, yourself," replied Father Small, hoping to move the conversation on to another topic.

"Yes," replied Father Strong. "God has been very generous to me and from what I have heard, to you as well. I was pleasantly surprised to hear of your appointment as Rector of the seminary. Your work in the seminary must have impressed the bishop very much to be placed in such a position of responsibility as a first assignment."

"Well, the bishop wanted someone with fresh ideas to prepare the candidates for the priesthood. Someone not too steeped in the old ways," replied Father Small arrogantly.

"Oh... well... come and see the church," said Father Strong, preferring not to hear him relate more of the bishop's reasons for completely overhauling the Seminary. That, in fact, was just one of the many major changes in the two years since the bishop's appointment.

"I'm sure it hasn't changed much since your boyhood days when your Aunt Cecilia would bring you here in the summer for Mass. Although it may look a little different, since just last week we finished our renovation project."

"You know of my summer visits to Aunt Cecilia?" questioned Father Small, a little surprised at Father Strong's knowledge of his boyhood.

"Yes," answered Father Strong. "I got to know your aunt quite well before she passed away last year. I would take her Communion every Sunday afternoon and then we would often have long conversations. She was a very fine woman and very generous to the poor. The building where we have our soup kitchen and homeless shelter was donated by her; but I'm sure you knew that."

"No, actually I didn't," replied Father Small. "I hadn't seen much of her over the past years."

They made their way down the long hall from the rectory to the Church, and as they entered the vestibule Father Strong was reminded by a poster hanging there of the coming week's activities. He tried to turn the topic of conversation to one he hoped would be more appealing to Father Small.

"We are beginning a Forty-Hour Devotion this coming Sunday night. Father Cozang will be here as the homilist. He always has an inspiring message for the people."

Responding in a voice of contempt that was not too well hidden, Father Small said, "Oh, Father Cozang! He is very traditional, isn't he? I've always found him to be quite closed minded, but then that has just been my experience."

Realizing that he may have been a little too openly blunt with his remarks, Father Small quickly attempted to change the topic of conversation by asking, "What else do you have going on in the parish?"

"Well," began Father Strong thoughtfully, "besides our outreach programs like the soup kitchen and Pregnancy Help, we have Vespers on Sunday evenings, daily Mass, Bible study on Tuesday evenings, R.C.I.A. on Wednesday evenings, and Stations of the Cross on Friday evenings."

"I didn't hear you mention RENEW, haven't you started it yet?" questioned Father Small.

"No, I don't think we will be doing that," answered the older priest.

"Why?" demanded Father Small. "It has opened so many people's minds."

"I was rather skeptical of it from the first time I heard of it," answered Father Strong. "It seemed to me that bringing a dozen lay-people together to discuss a book full of rather leading questions without adequate supervision might not be the most responsible approach to enlightening my parishioners about the faith. And after praying over it and hearing some disturbing reports on it from several places where it had been tried, I decided against it."

"You don't think your parishioners could come together to form a consensus about the faith that would be good?" questioned Father Small.

Patiently, Father Strong explained, "I think more than good intentions are necessary for one to come to a knowledge of the truth. People's consciences must be properly formed in the truth. The Church is not a democracy where a vote of the people will decide what is truth. God is the source of truth; it is not dormant within man waiting to be discovered. Throughout the ages, God has revealed His truth primarily through His Holy Word and the Church.

"If we are going to encourage people to be better informed in the faith, then I believe we have a responsibility to ensure that the true faith is being presented. It is all too easy for a strong-willed person with an improperly formed faith to come into a small group and lead it astray. This is exactly what has been happening in other parishes where RENEW has been implemented."

Beaming red in the face, Father Small protested, "But, Father Strong, the bishop is very supportive of RENEW."

"Yes, I know," continued Father Strong, "I have spoken to him several times concerning the program and have tried to warn him of the dangers involved with it. We all very much need to grow in our understanding of the faith, but from what I have seen, RENEW holds much more potential for spreading confusion than for building faith."

As they entered the church, Father Small now seemed bent on looking for an area to trip-up the older priest, as he questioned, "I see that you have done much work here, in painting the whole interior and resurfacing all the wooden surfaces. But why in doing all of this did you not remove the altar rail at that time, instead of wasting time and money refinishing it? And, I see that your tabernacle is still located in the center of the back wall behind the altar, wouldn't it have been easier to have moved it to a less noticeable location while you were renovating the church?"

"The people are really quite pleased with the sanctuary as it is," answered Father Strong. "It inspires them to pray and worship God. Most people say they feel close to God when they are here. Having been built nearly one hundred years ago, this church is nearly the same as it was when many of their grandparents were children. This building is like a comforting, old friend to many of our parishioners."

Father Small retorted, "But surely, Father, you have read the National Council of Catholic Bishop's letter, *Art and Environment in American Worship*, that mandates several changes in church form which you have not addressed here."

"I am very familiar with the letter of which you speak," he answered, beginning to feel as though Father Small had visited him to critique his performance. "The letter of which you speak was prepared by one of their councils but was never approved by the Bishops. It has no force of authority behind it. It is only one small group's narrow, and I might add harmful, opinion."

"What makes you say that?" commanded Father Small with his voice becoming noticeably shaky.

"There were enough valid changes after Vatican Council II for the people to assimilate," continued Father Strong. "The excessive and uncalled for changes have only succeeded in confusing many Catholics. Many of the unauthorized changes that have been implemented have decreased the people's awareness of Almighty God's presence in our worship.

"So many of those changes attempt to place our attention back upon ourselves. We have all week long to observe and reflect upon humanity. Surely one hour a week is not asking too much time to center our thoughts on God and worship Him."

"Then you believe in a religion that is just between God and me?" insisted Father Small, sternly.

"No," disagreed Father Strong. "We must, of course, recognize our brothers and sisters in Christ, but what I am saying, and in fact what the Church has said down through the centuries, is that we primarily come together at Mass to worship the Almighty. The believers gather together at Mass to center their thoughts, prayers and worship upon the One, True God. What has been promoted in so many places is an environment where entirely too much attention is placed upon the assembly of believers and not enough upon the Almighty."

"Vatican II called upon the changes, Father, not I," pleaded Father Small.

Father Strong corrected, "No, that is not the case at all. Read the Documents of Vatican II. They make very few changes in our way of worship. Almost all of the changes have been made through the teachings of so-called experts who have went way beyond the Documents with their personal agendas for change. Whenever anyone comes up with their own idea of improvement in environment or liturgy, all they do is say, 'This was mandated by the Council,' and they force its implementation upon a parish.

"I have personally seen many examples of this perversion of Vatican II that is running so rampant in the Church. This spirit of change for the sake of change has allowed serious deviations of the faith to creep in. We must be careful, especially for the sake of those who are weak in the faith. When we change enough of the relatively minor things and do not properly teach the people, we give the impression that everything is subject to change, even the basic Doctrines of the Church."

"And how would you know what it would be that you might change, assuming you would ever change anything?" shot back Father Small.

"I would look to what the bishops in union with the Holy Father, the Pope, were saying," answered Father Strong. "I would search the Word of God, the writings of the saints, and most surely I would pray earnestly to Almighty God for guidance."

"Well, I, and many others in the Church today, disagree with you," came the harsh words from Father Small. "What is needed in today's fast moving, modern world is action, not more people sitting around praying while the world passes them by.

"Looking to the saints for guidance, in my estimation, is a waste of time. If we look toward any group as an example for us today it should be the movers and shakers of our own age. Those people who have come up against a corrupt system and have beaten it should be our models. That is

The New Age

definitely the direction we will be taking from here on out at the Seminary. Modern tools for the modern priest."

"It saddens me to hear you say that," replied Father Strong with a heavy heart. "When I heard of your appointment I prayed that you could return the seminary back into an instrument truly preparing priests to witness to Jesus as they went out into the world, but you seem to be promoting ways that are popular with the world."

"Come on, Father," retorted Father Small, "this is the modern world that we are in. People will not listen to the old ways any longer. You will have to get used to that or retire and let a younger man who can handle the changes take your place. New ways are needed in the modern world. It's not the old world any more. This is a New Age!"

Father Strong was obviously quite disappointed in his brother priest but tried to explain, "People are the same as they have always been. They still have the same old basic needs and, I might add, basic sins."

"Sins!" sneered Father Small.

"You don't believe sin is a question here?" asked a bewildered Father Strong.

"Well, it has been enlightening talking with you," snapped Father Small, as he abruptly turned and strutted toward the entrance of the church. "I really must be leaving if I am to make it to Glory Falls in time for dinner with the Bishop."

Father Strong genuflected to the Lord's presence in the tabernacle and followed Father Small to the front of the church. But, Father Small was already in his car and pulling away from the curb.

With that, Revealael opened Peter's eyes to see two other beings within the church vestibule. They were two that he readily recognized, Kolar and Goolar. They seemed to be quite proud of the achievements they had accomplished there.

"I see that, once again, I can report to lord Lucifer that I have carried out his plans brilliantly," boasted Kolar. "Your name will be mentioned, of course."

"O most wise Primary, thank you," whined Goolar. "We have managed quite nicely to cause division within the Enemy's ranks. Attacking the very heart of the Enemy's Church was a very wise decision on your part."

"Yes," replied a proud Kolar, "I knew if we were persistent we could turn Vatican II's minor changes into a hellish movement of change against their Church. We have successfully taken the thoughts of many of the best of them away from the Enemy and placed it upon the altar of change. I lust it greatly. I'm such a genius."

"O great Primary, you are truly worthy," returned Goolar, groveling to his superior. "Now that we have such a good start within the Church, where should we specifically go from here?"

"First of all, keep up your efforts at causing change. That, as we have seen, is a very effective way to bring about division and, above all, it takes their thoughts away from the Enemy.

"I think we also need to follow through on this democracy in the Church concept. Any ground we can gain in the battle to get them to think that morality and doctrine can be best decided by a popular vote will indeed be a victory for our kingdom of darkness. It is a good plan, and this is the age for it. This concept fits in beautifully with our attempt to center their thoughts upon themselves and away from the Enemy.

"Possibly another fertile area to explore would be in encouraging the use of committees in their Church. I know that in some rare cases this might actually help their awful cause, but our latest research has shown that overall we stand to gain significantly from their use of committees in governing the local parish. The important thing to remember about this approach is that the most active members will spend much of their time in useless committee babble when they would otherwise be doing something productive for the Enemy.

"I am especially pleased by the inroads we have made into their seminaries. What we have accomplished there is a good example of what can be done to counteract the best of the Enemy's plans if we but patiently work to move the silly humans down the wrong track. Still, there is much more that we could be doing.

"We must continue to work hard at the seminaries. The priests are key players in the defeat of their Church. If we pervert the faith of one lay person, he may bring with him one or two others. If we can pervert the faith of one priest he will bring with him human fodder by the hundreds or thousands!

"Keep encouraging them to look to the movers of this age and not to their history and saints. Remember one of lord Lucifer's favorite sayings 'To encourage ignorance of the past is to encourage repeating its mistakes.'

"And above all else, encourage them to act rather than pray. This is an important part of our plan. If they don't spend time with the Enemy, listening to his instruction, how will they work in any kind of an effective way to accomplish His plans?

"With their efforts taking them round and round in circles, they will help us build up Lucifer's kingdom of darkness without ever knowing it. Together we will truly usher in a New Age."

With those discouraging words, the demons disappeared and Peter turned to Revealael to ask, "This has really opened my eyes to what has been happening around me, but what can be done about it? Can those who claim to be Christian be made to see what is really happening in the world and overcome the demons' plans?"

Without hesitation the angel firmly replied, "We know where the only power comes from that can transform the world. It comes from the Lord Jesus. Only through the grace flowing from the One that conquered sin and death can the world find the means to reform. Only through Jesus can mankind come to the Father and find fulfillment.

"Every person has grave need to repent and turn to Him. Yet, people like to keep themselves at the center of their lives. They will not easily turn away from self and turn to the only One who can save them.

"But don't give up hope; by no means is all lost. For what may seem impossible to man is just a doorway of opportunity for God. Yes, with God all things are possible."

CHAPTER 12

The New Church

"*I* have taken you into the past to see all that you were destined to see," proclaimed Revealael. "What you have seen is by no means everything that is important, only what you personally needed to understand. I can say no more about that.

"You also need to better understand what is happening in your own time. Things are not always as they appear, nor as we wish they might be. The evil ones have a powerful foothold in this world. They are attempting to turn Christ's Church into a new church built in their image. We will now go to where you can see just how broadly their influence has spread."

Peter waited in anticipation for the dark clouds to roll in, but surprisingly, they did not come. Instead of clouds, total darkness touched him, blacking out his mind for a moment. His comprehension of space and time had been momentarily taken from him, and when it returned, Peter found that he and Revealael were in a luxuriously furnished office.

There behind a beautifully crafted, oak desk was a middle-aged man sitting in a plush leather chair. Peter recognized him immediately as Bishop Bill. It wasn't too difficult; probably half the people within the diocese's boundary could recognize him at a glance. Rightly so, for his picture had been in the local paper, for one reason or another, nearly every week for the past three years since his appointment as bishop of the Glory Falls Diocese.

Yes, Bishop William R. Small, preferring to be called Bishop Bill, had quite an ability to make the news. Good news, bad news, any news, it made no difference. The one constant seemed to be that it was always the serious-minded Catholics who were the most scandalized.

After all that Peter had heard about the bishop, he felt as though he knew him personally, even though he believed he had never been in the same building with him. And then it dawned on him, Peter realized something that had not realized before. Bishop Bill was an older Father Small. He was the same Father Small whom Peter had witnessed in the past visiting the good Father Strong.

Suddenly, the office door opened and a young priest stepped in and quickly closed the door behind him as if he was afraid of being followed. "Bishop," he said excitedly, "they still will not leave. What should I do? They have been out there for over two hours, and despite all my efforts I still cannot convince them to leave."

"Paul, can't you get them to come back tomorrow? Tell them anything; just get them out of here," insisted the bishop.

"I've already tried everything I could think of," said Father Paul. "They are just as determined as they were earlier, and they claim they are going to stay until you speak with them, no matter how long it takes."

The bishop, losing his normal calm composure, snarled, "Those miserable misfits. Of all the days for them to show up, they have to plant their carcasses here on the day Congressman Hank is coming!"

"Well, I could call the police and have them removed," suggested Father Paul.

"No! No!" interjected the bishop, and he quickly waved his hands back and forth in the air. "We've got enough problems, as it is, without having that plastered on the front page of the paper. It's already difficult keeping federal money coming in to support our projects. We can't risk losing our support through a few fanatics getting us in the news."

"Alright, just tell them whatever it takes to get rid of them," chimed in Father Paul.

"Exactly!" agreed the bishop as Father Paul headed towards the door.

In a few minutes Father Paul returned with two women and a man, "Bishop, this is Jan Brown and Betty and Floyd Kruger. As I informed you, they have some things that have been troubling them very much which they would like to bring to your attention."

In near unison the three visitors replied, "Good afternoon, Bishop Small."

"Please, come sit down and make yourselves comfortable," replied the Bishop. "And please, call me Bishop Bill, after all, we are all part of the Lord's family here. I assume you have been introduced to Father Paul Drey, my secretary. He prefers to be called Father Paul, if you please.

"I am really very sorry that you had to wait so long to see me, but you must understand that I am kept so busy that it is sometimes hard for me to take time for anything unscheduled during the day. The postponement of an appointment for this afternoon has given me a spare twenty minutes that I am most happy to share with you. So do begin. I am most interested in hearing about what is troubling you."

"We apologize for barging in on you, Bishop Bill, but we have written to you three times and have never received a reply. We were at a loss for what else to do," replied Betty.

"Were your letters addressed directly to me?" asked the bishop.

"Yes," replied Betty.

"I never received them," claimed the Bishop. "No one else should be getting the mail that is personally addressed to me. I don't understand, but I'll get to the bottom of this, you can be sure."

Turning to his side where Father Paul was seated, he gave a slight wink to him as he said, "Father Paul, please make a memo to the administration office for me. Tell them I want them to positively ensure that I receive all mail that is personally addressed to me.

"I'm sorry, Betty, please continue, and Paul, would you please record their concerns so that we don't forget anything."

"We come from Blessed Virgin Parish, up in Riverton," said Betty, somewhat nervous but under control. "We have been concerned for some time about the things that Father Moe Cykle has been doing since he came to the parish two years ago. We have spoken to him on many occasions, but the situation has only gotten worse.

"When he first arrived at the parish it seemed that Father Moe was on a schedule of changing one or two things every week. They are much the same as the liturgical deviations that seem to be going on in a lot of other parishes too, so I imagine you've heard much of this before.

"Well anyway, it started out with things like having the people sit and stand at times other than what is proper to the order of the Mass, having the choir sing a totally unrelated song in place of the Psalm, and having himself and the Eucharistic ministers receive Communion after the congregation.

"And, of course, it didn't stop there. He had the choir quit singing the Gloria, and soon it was omitted altogether. He also refused to say the Creed, and yes, I'm talking about on Sundays. All this was just the beginning.

"Several of us spoke to him on several occasions about what he was doing. I mean, after all, if the Church has a specific way to celebrate the Mass, who is one person to change it on his own? But at that point in time, Father Moe was so forceful that he convinced us that the Conference of Bishops was in the process of changing all these things. He said that what he was doing was just in anticipation of changes that had already been approved.

"Needless to say, we were quite ignorant then. As time went on he pushed into areas where he was so blatantly in error that we woke up. Soon he was changing the Scripture readings at Mass to suit him and his assistant, Sister Jane. It became a terrible infraction of their perverted scripture to say the word 'man.' Even when the Scripture obviously applied to Jesus they would change it to person, or human being, or some other equally awkward replacement.

"If there is a problem with some people's understanding of a word why can't the priest explain it in his homily? Wouldn't that make the most sense? Tell the people that in the beginning the Book of Genesis says that, 'God made man, male and female he made them.' Wouldn't that be a lot easier than changing the Word of God, as though God didn't know what He was doing?"

"That wasn't the worst of it," interjected Jan. "They began to change other passages of the Scriptures as well, like 'homosexual acts' became 'unloving relationships,' and 'obeying the commandments' even became 'following your conscience.' It just kept going further and further away from the reality of God's Word."

"Several of us went and talked to Father Moe about this," continued Betty. "We tried to calmly explain our position to him, but he would have none of it. And so, I asked him about the Church's Cannon number 825. It says that translations of Scripture must be approved by the Apostolic See or the Episcopal Conference.

"Father Moe became raving mad, even using profane language. He told us that since we had not been trained in Cannon Law that we had no business trying to read it. He said that he knew what he was doing and that we had no business being critical of the Scripture he used.

"Seeing how upset he had become, we left without saying any more. It was at that time that we first decided to write to you, and so we did."

"Again," offered the bishop, and he shrugged his shoulders, "I apologize for the error of my staff in losing your letter, but please do continue."

"From then on, probably because we were now more sensitive, things seemed to go downhill by leaps and bounds. Father Moe even began to freely replace parts of the Eucharistic Prayers with words of his own. Even to the point of using a pop song in place of the liturgy.

"He set up various councils to help him run the Church. That would have been fine if he would have provided training for their members, but he didn't. Some of his choices for members on these councils were totally unbelievable. Now, I know it would be easy to say, 'Well that is just "sour-grapes" speaking because you weren't chosen,' so let me give you an example: The chairman of the Pastoral Council is an outspoken member of Catholics for a Free-Choice, that group that promotes abortion, the same one that Rome has condemned on several occasions!

"It was this same Pastoral Council that brought us the speaker for our Forty-Hour Devotion last year. You know whom they chose? The laicized priest, Gabriel Baear, who was long ago censured by Rome and has been forbidden to speak at any Catholic function. He is very big into New Age Religions, especially worship of the earth. So, you know what we heard for three evenings? The spirituality of mother earth! It was at this time that we sent you our second letter.

"Then, of course, there's the once-a-month exhibition of sister Jane reading the Gospel and giving the homily at the weekend Masses. Most of them are too dry and poorly given to take much notice of, although some stand out, like the time she called the Pope a 'dried-up old fossil,' for saying that it was impossible for women to ever be ordained to holy orders.

"The third letter we sent because of what was going on in our parish school. The School Council that Father Moe personally selected deemed it appropriate to bring in the 'Diamond' group to teach the children sex education. This program was for students all the way down to the first-grade. I don't know if you are familiar with it, but it is quite an explicitly detailed, and I might add, secular, program. It is one hour a day for five weeks.

"The sex-education program was kept pretty quiet. Some of us found out they were giving explicit instruction in deviant sexual acts, but when they handed out condoms to all the students in the fifth grade and above, everyone heard of it. Several of us called Father Moe, but he flatly refused to speak to us about this program. When I approached him after Mass one morning, he simply said, 'You don't have children in school. It's not your concern.' Then, to a friend of mine, who does have children in the school, he simply said, 'That's the way it is, if you don't like it then put your children in another school.' Now I ask you, what kind of a Christian attitude is that?

"There is always something new being presented in the parish that is opposed to Church teaching. Last week in his Sunday homily, Father Moe said we should all be ashamed because our Church has not yet recognized 'homosexual marriages.' He actually said that we are responsible for giving homosexuals an inferiority complex.

"I think that I've said enough, although the deviations from Church teaching just go on and on. To help you confirm our story we have compiled a list of specific incidents with dates and names for you. I have people's phone numbers listed so you can check out their story, if you wish."

"Here you go Bishop," offered Floyd in a low voice as he handed over the list.

"Thank you very much," replied the Bishop, quickly receiving the list and displaying an air of great interest. "I am very concerned about what I hear going on. I will investigate all that you have told me and then take it to the Presbyteral Council for discernment.

"For now though, please excuse me. My free time is nearly used up. I have to leave soon for a meeting concerning our Diocesan outreach programs. Rest assured that I am very sympathetic to the situation at Blessed Virgin Parish and will be taking decisive action soon."

"Thank you for your time, Bishop," said Floyd, who was quickly joined in respectful appreciation by Jan and Betty. Smiling faces and handshakes went around the room, as the

The New Church

three visitors were gently, but firmly, encouraged out the door by Father Paul.

In a few moments Father Paul reentered the bishop's office with right thumb up, and proclaimed, "Great job, Bill. You got rid of them just like you said you would. But what are you going to do when they see that your actions don't show that you sympathize with them?"

"I'll send them a transcript of this meeting. If you think closely, I never said that I sympathized with them, but rather with the situation at their parish, and I do. I think they are a real pain to Moe Cykle."

"Excellent," replied Father Paul with a laugh. "What do you want me to do with my notes and their list?"

"Just file them away for now," answered the Bishop.

"Won't you need them for the Presbyteral Council?"

"No. I have no intention of bringing that trash up at the Council," said the bishop forcefully. "I do intend to inform the council of the situation at Blessed Virgin Parish, as I see it. I'll ask for suggestions on what we can do to keep extremist parishioners in line."

"You thoroughly amaze me," remarked Father Paul admiringly.

"Yes," replied Bishop Bill in a teasing voice, "I believe you've told me that before."

Their conversation was interrupted by the sound of the doorbell. When Father Paul returned from answering the door, Congressman Herbert Hank entered with him.

"Hello, Herbert," said the bishop as he held out his hand to greet the congressman. "How is everything going in Washington these days?"

"Good to see you, Bishop," replied Herbert with a tired voice, as he took his hand. "Not so well, actually. With all the push for cuts in spending, it's a real rat race down there.

A person just doesn't know what those darn Republicans are going to come up with next."

"All this isn't going to cut into any of the programs that we have worked on, is it?" questioned a concerned Bishop Bill.

"Well," continued Herbert, trying to ease into the bad news, "some of the social programs are going to have to go. Many programs will be greatly reduced. Some may remain nearly at their current level, but across the board there are going to be major cuts in spending."

"Now Herbert," protested the Bishop. "You know very well that 75 to 80% of our funding is from federal monies. I have a lot of friends who are going to loose their jobs if we have to cut back on our federally funded programs.

"It wouldn't look very good for me. I'm young yet, plenty of time to be Archbishop, maybe even Cardinal, one day. I can't afford to hurt my friends. You're a man of the world, Herbert; you know how it is."

"Yes, of course, Bishop," squirmed Herbert, knowing what was coming, "I feel for your situation, I really do."

"I'm sure you do," consoled the bishop. "Across the board cuts can be very devastating. They could cause an organization like ours to also make widespread cuts in its spending. You know, everything from building construction to campaign contributions would probably have to be cut. I sure would hate to see that happen. It would be especially disheartening in cases, like your own, where a politician has worked so hard for us in the past."

"I'll try my best, Bishop Bill," pleaded Herbert, "but I just don't know how much I can do."

"That is all we can ask for, Herbert," replied the Bishop.

"Well, I really do need to be going to the airport now to pick up Senator Budd and Congressman Kramer who are flying in and spending the weekend at my resort on the lake," revealed Hank, a well-known homosexual. "But, I will use this opportunity to inform them of your situation. Maybe they will have some ideas on how we could preserve your funding."

"Very well," encouraged the Bishop, "keep up the effort."

"You know, Bishop, you are welcome at any time to come and visit us at the resort," offered Herbert. Then, not sure of how the Bishop would take his offer, added, "I mean, we have several guesthouses and the view there along the lake is truly beautiful. It might be good for you to get away from all your responsibilities for a few days at a time, now and then."

"Yes, that does sound very good, Herbert," agreed Bishop Bill, "We will definitely have to take you up on that generous offer."

"You will?" blurted Herbert, quite surprised. "I mean, that's good, very good."

"Don't be so surprised, Herbert," interjected Father Paul, with a grin on his face, "Bishop Bill is very liberal minded. We will most certainly come over some time. In fact, several times over the years we have talked about how good it would be to get away to a place like yours." And then, with a wink, he added, "I understand you host some very lively parties."

"Why, yes!" agreed Herbert, now somewhat relieved and smiling. "I will be sure to invite you both to the next party that I have. And you know, the more I think about it, I am confident that my friends in congress and I will come up with a way to keep your funds coming. I'm not sure just how yet, but don't you worry about a thing. Just leave everything to Ol' Herbie."

The three shook hands, and Congressman Hank was on his way out when Father Paul, noticing the time, said, "We had better get going, Bill. We've just enough time to change, grab our bags, and get to the airport before the plane leaves."

"Right, Paul, I'm ready for a vacation." agreed the Bishop.

"Imagine," said Father Paul, as he gently took the Bishop's hand, "you and me alone in the Caribbean for six wonderful days!"

With that, Peter's awareness turned upon a more commanding presence that suddenly became apparent within the room, as he heard a now-familiar Kolar begin to speak.

"Surely, you have performed an excellent service to the kingdom, Goolar, and I assure you that it will not be forgotten. Yours shall be of the most prime distraction that the kingdom has to offer.

"You have truly worked out a lustful combination of power and perverted sex in the midst of the Enemy's Church, as is demonstrated by these two. Ah, just think of the grief that they must cause the Enemy!"

"Thank you, great Primary," sniveled Goolar. "The great beauty in this attack is that it is growing daily by leaps and bounds. We have already coerced a large number of the Enemy's priests into our camp. Most of them don't even realize it, of course, and that is the real beauty of it. So full of rationalizing pride, they believe that because the enemy loves them He will overlook whatever they do. What simple-minded morons. Isn't pride wonderful?"

"Ha! It has always worked quite good for my purposes," sneered the Primary. "But lets move on. This is such great distraction; I want to witness a few more examples."

The demons vanished and Peter questioned Revealael, "I know that we are all sinners, but how could so many priests, and even bishops, follow such evil ways?"

"You are justified in asking questions about such circumstances," reassured Revealael. "For although all mankind commits sinful acts, Christ's priests have been given special grace and they are called to a higher accounting than other men. It is truly sad, but a large number have fallen away, thus abandoning the faith.

"In seeking to please themselves more than God, they have chosen the so-called wisdom of the world over the wisdom of God. They have grown ashamed of the gospel of Jesus, and have exchanged it for a sugary gospel that the world will accept. But only the true Gospel has the power to save. What they have been proclaiming has only led them further into derision.

"They will not tolerate sound doctrine because it opposes the life they have been living. It exposes their sins. Adding sin upon sin, they have fallen deeply into the darkness. Now they prefer the darkness to the light because their deeds are evil and they do not want them revealed. Pray that they will repent and return to the one, true faith.

"Still, although their number may be great, there are a larger number of Christ's priests who are faithful to the Gospel of He who called them. Rejoice and take comfort in the holy and faithful leaders within the Church, they are as Christ for you. Pray especially hard for them, for they face not only the obstacles of the evil ones and the world, but also the terrible burden and pain that comes from their fellow priests who proclaim a false Gospel.

"You must understand that at this time there are in the middle of those two groups a large number of priests who are experiencing a great struggle in differentiating between the Kingdom of God and the kingdom of darkness. They want to do what is good and right but are greatly influenced by that which is not of God. They are easily led astray by their fellow priests who prefer the darkness. Pray earnestly for them that they may find the wisdom and strength in Christ Jesus to faithfully serve Him. He alone is worthy."

CHAPTER 13

The Grief and the Glory

Deeply disturbed by what he had seen happening, Peter asked Revealael, "What is to become of the Church?"

Solemnly the angel warned, "The problems within the Church must be squarely faced, or they will linger on to cause the destruction of many souls. Problems exist in and have a consuming control over the general society, but battling the evil within the Church is much more crucial. After all, it is Christ's Church that holds the keys to the Kingdom; it has been entrusted with the Good News of Salvation!

"The Church has always been made up of sinners, but these are no small matters of occasional sin that we now find running rampant. In this age sin is often ignored or manipulated in self-righteous justification. Especially disheartening is the degree to which many priests and bishops have fallen into the snares of the devil."

"With the blind leading the blind, how will anyone find their way?" asked Peter.

"Unless many hear the call of the Spirit, repent, and turn to the Lord, there will be much pain and grief for the Church," replied Revealael. "Unfortunately there are far too many in the Church who have repressed the voice of the Spirit through unrepentant sin. If hearts remain hardened and the situation progresses at its present course, there will be much to suffer."

Deeply moved, Peter asked, "Then the present situation can be corrected?"

"Yes, of course," answered Revealael. "Though local portions may fall, Jesus has promised that His Spirit would preserve the Church until the end of time. Where God is found so too is hope.

"Now, I will show you what is to come. This will not be as before when we were actually present in the past and you experienced what could not be changed. Now, it has been granted for you to see visions of the future. First, you will see what could likely happen in the future, and then, of what will surely come to pass."

Revealael gently placed his hands palm side down upon the top of Peter's head. A warm comforting sensation flowed from the angel into Peter. Then, Revealael commanded, "Close your eyes and see!"

Within Peter's mind a vision appeared. A red-faced priest stood at the doorway of an unknown church. He was pointing toward some people who were kneeling within the church. Then, police officers dragged one person after another from the sanctuary of the church. Those being ejected did not attempt to fight back. Their only offense seemed to be the fact that they were in the church praying.

One man proclaimed as he was drug past the angry priest, "We will not turn our backs on the Word of God. You will never force us to accept the false scriptures that you have concocted!"

Another vision appeared. In it was a room with one large door. On one side of the door was a long line of men, young and old. They said they had come to answer their call to the priesthood, but the keeper of the door would not let them through. The keeper said they were not fit to be priests because their minds were rigid and closed since they did not accept the lifestyles of all people.

Within the room, a bishop was attempting to ordain several women into the priesthood. At the end of the ceremony, the bishop congratulated them and said this was a great day for the Church—a new age!

Outside, a group of two-dozen people who had been kneeling on the sidewalk and praying the Rosary were being thrown into a police wagon. Their crime, it seems, was praying for the salvation of those who were inside.

The hideous face of a demon appeared, laughing on and on with a frighteningly evil sound. Finally, he stopped and boasted, "With all these filthy lovers of truth gone the church will be ours to do with as we please!"

A newspaper appeared and its headline read, "Bishop uses embezzled money to support lavish gay lifestyle," while the sobbing of thousands upon thousands of people could be heard. Immediately thereafter, Peter saw a vision of tears flowing down the streets of the city in a stream that grew higher with the passing of time until bodies were seen being washed away in its current.

After that, the voices of a multitude of angels in heaven could be heard petitioning, "Almighty Lord, say but the word and we shall avenge your Holy Name, for the sanctuary of your Church has become an open dwelling place for perversion. Lust and greed are proudly displayed to the nations of the world."

Other newspapers appeared and their headlines boldly proclaimed, "Rome declares American Catholic Bishops to be in schism," and "American Catholic Church splits from

Rome." Then, Peter saw many bishops and a multitude of priests dancing in wild abandon with a horde of demons.

Soon, a courtroom appeared. Those gathered within it were deciding the fate of the Church's property. One lawyer demanded that Rome maintain title. He said, "It is Church Law that Church property is to be administered by the bishop whom the Pope has rightfully appointed to the diocese; it has never been recognized otherwise."

A second lawyer argued that the property should stay with the bishop who broke away from Rome and what he claimed was the majority of the people of the diocese. His claim rested on the fact that America was a nation of the people. He insisted that Church law and what other nations had done did not apply, as America was under no law greater than its own.

Another vision appeared. It was of a pasture full of sheep. The sheep were confused and scared, wandering in every direction. They could not see or hear their shepherd. They did not know which way to go.

On the far end of the pasture several wolves killed some of the sheep and put on their skin for clothing. Then they picked up sticks and made themselves look as if they were bishops with their crosiers. They called to the sheep and many followed. The sheep were lead over a hill to where a large pack of hungry wolves awaited them. The wolves surrounded them, devouring them one by one.

Then, at the other end of the pasture appeared their True Shepherd. He was dressed as a bishop with miter and cozier, and his voice sounded like the roar of rushing waters. He was visible to all, and called out to His sheep.

Many of the sheep followed the false shepherds and were destroyed, but others followed the True Shepherd. For though they had been very confused, once they could clearly hear and see the two choices, they recognized the True Shepherd and followed Him.

At that moment, from outside of the world passing before his mind, Peter heard Revealael command, "Now, you shall see that which will without doubt come to be!"

Immediately, Peter saw the sun burning brightly like a huge, fiery ball. He looked closely and saw an angel standing upon its surface. The angel grew larger and larger until the sun became as a mere stepping stone to him, and his brightness outshone that of the sun.

The angel raised a giant trumpet and blew it three times so loudly that it shook the very stars in the sky. When the stars settled back into their original position, the angel cried out in a voice as loud as the trumpet blast, "Behold, inhabitants of the earth, rejoice and tremble; the day has arrived for the return of the Lord of Creation!"

There then appeared on the face of the earth two vast armies. They each numbered in the thousands upon thousands and millions upon millions. They were engaged in fierce combat throughout all the nations and peoples of the earth.

Peter noticed, though, that those who were most involved in the battle were not human; they were angels and demons, and the weapons that they fought with were not bullets and bombs, but were ideas and words. Most of the humans seemed oblivious to the nature of the battle raging around them. They struggled and fought for survival, but they seemed not to know who was the enemy they were fighting or who it was that was helping them in their battle. In fact, they had been so long into the battle that iniquity and chaos had become accepted by them as normalcy.

The angel who was standing upon the sun again shouted, "Today is the day. Now, while the inhabitants of the earth are congratulating themselves on the world they have made and shouting 'Peace, peace,' where there is no peace, will the end come upon them. Like a thief in the night will He, who must come, come unexpectedly to them."

Again the angel blew the trumpet. This time it was much louder than before, so loud that even the inhabitants of the earth heard it. The stars in the sky pulled back away from the earth, and the heavens broke open with a loud roar, as the Sign of the Son of Man appeared.

A brilliant cross that was twenty times larger than the full moon came forth from the opening in the heavens. Somehow it appeared in the eastern sky to every point on the face of the earth all at one time. The inhabitants of the earth were awestruck, but not for long.

The angel who was standing on the sun declared, "Now has all here come to an end, for time is no more!"

Out of the opening in the heavens came One riding upon a white horse. His name was King of kings and Lord of lords, and His glory was beyond all compare. Behind him came all the armies of heaven. There were thousands and thousands of angels, swooping down upon the earth with golden wings unfurled. In their right hands they brandished two-edged swords on which were engraved, "Word of God," and they shouted as in one voice, "The Lord of Glory comes!"

The King spoke but a Word, and the bodies of those who had died in His friendship miraculously came out from the depths of the earth and sea. They were no longer corruptible but were suddenly incorruptible and glorious in their perfection. They rose to the One seated on the white horse where he reunited them to the souls for which they belonged.

The Grief and the Glory

Again the King of Glory spoke and a third of His angels were dispatched to the earth. They collected the elect who were living. In the twinkling of an eye they too were transformed into glorious beings and joined the King of kings.

Welcoming them into His presence, He said, "Welcome my beloved and faithful servants into the kingdom that has been prepared for you. Together we will reign forever and ever."

The Lord spoke again and another third of His angels departed, collected Lucifer and all the demons, and threw them into the everlasting pit that had been prepared for them. There, in their sin, they will burn forever.

Then, there appeared a great white throne on which the King of Glory sat with His chosen ones. All who ever lived on the earth knelt in His presence as He opened the Book of Deeds, and the works of all were made known.

Another Book was opened—the Book of Life. Anyone whose name was not written in the Book of Life was thrown into the eternal pit that had been prepared for the demons, and there they will dwell in their sin forever.

Suddenly, there appeared a new heaven and a new earth as the old ones disappeared. The angel who formerly stood on the sun now stood upon the new earth announcing, "Behold the Kingdom of God. Now will His people remain with Him forever and ever. Never feeling pain nor sorrow, they shall share the dwelling of their Brother Jesus in their Father's house."

And Peter saw joy and love everywhere. Perfect fulfillment abounded. Nothing was hidden or withheld within God's dwelling. All were as one, and yet, all beheld total joy and love for each other, for God had removed every trace of jealousy, greed and fear from them. Wherever

Peter looked, he could find nothing that was not good and pleasing and holy.

So many wondrous things Peter could not understand, and yet, he knew that he never wanted this vision to leave him. The joy upon the faces of those who were there was enough to convince him of the unimaginable wonder of heaven. He didn't have to totally understand being within the presence of God to see that it was more than he had ever dreamed possible.

He realized that to fully know God was more than his limited, human mind could comprehend. How foolish he had been to question God's ways. Seeing only a small glimpse of heavenly glory was more than enough to convince him that God's ways are vastly above what man could now understand.

"Yes," he thought, "in looking through my small understanding of heaven, I see that faith is the only way possible to approach God. Only like a little child trusting in their parent as they take their first step, can one begin to approach God."

It was then that Peter felt the hands of Revealael lift from his head and the vision ended. He had wanted desperately for the vision to remain, but Peter was not sorrowful. On the contrary, he was overflowing with extreme joy and thankfulness for being allowed to see what he had seen.

Though he had been filled with confusion before meeting Revealael, he now felt confident in God's providence. Above all, he knew that he wanted to reach faith's goal of life on high in Christ Jesus.

Tears of joy began to flow from Peter's eyes as he thought of how much love God must hold for man to have prepared such heavenly wonders for him. A Bible verse which he had often heard, but never really understood, came to his mind: "Eye hath not seen, nor ear heard, neither have entered into the heart of man, the things which God hath prepared for them that love him."

Nothing on earth could ever begin to compare with what he had seen. No grief, pain, or ridicule the world could give would be too great to endure in the struggle to reach the reward for loving God.

AURORA ANGELS

CHAPTER 14

The Commission

Opening his eyes, Peter found himself back at Saint Alphonsus Church standing in front of the altar. The angel was at his side.

"Do you understand that better now?" asked Revealael while pointing at the crucifix hanging on the wall behind the altar.

"Yes," answered Peter. "So many things are clear now. Seeing the terrible result of sin, I see why it required such a precious offering. I'm sure I don't understand all the reasons God sent His Son to die for us, but paying such a great price for our redemption shows how horrible sin must be."

"You will do well to think often about the sacrifice that was offered for your salvation," recommended the angel. "Not acknowledging sin's seriousness is at the very heart of the problems in the world today.

"Encourage others to meditate on the holy image of the Savior upon the cross. For from that selfless act does flow grace sufficient to renew all of mankind. Through the death of the Lord Jesus, Almighty God built a bridge that man can cross to reach Him. This is the heart of the Good News. Share it freely."

Peter couldn't help but think of his earlier feelings. In a choked voice, he struggled to say, "I feel so blessed to have seen the visions of the glorious joys of heaven that you gave me, Revealael. Was I wrong in not ever wanting it to leave me?"

Placing a hand gently on Peter's shoulder, the angel consolingly offered, "No. I understand completely, and would feel the same way. It is the greatest good to desire God. No matter where I am or what I am doing I continuously behold God. It has to be this way for us angels. After experiencing the Almighty, we simply could not bear to be separated from Him. May the joy you have known guide you for the remainder of your life. Let your visions of the glory of God be a great strength to you. Above all, let Him be your heart's desire and surely you will dwell with Him forever."

"I never began to realize the great depth of heaven," continued Peter. "I mean, I wasn't of the same mind as those who make a joke of heaven, still, I never really gave heaven much thought beyond everyone there just standing around praising God. Now, I understand it as the unending joy in experiencing the unimaginable, awesome wonder of the infinite God!"

"If words could help you to understand more fully, I would speak them to you," replied Revealael. "No matter how hard one tries or with what analogies one uses, the understanding will always fall short of the reality of eternal life with God.

"As I told you before, even for the angels the Almighty God is continually like a refreshing breeze. I am always in great awe of Him. He is far beyond anything on earth you could attempt to compare Him to. Still, He calls me and loves me as though I were His only creation. Such is the

The Commission

great love of our God. He has this relationship with every holy angel and wishes it to be like this with every person.

"Peter, you have been granted a very special favor in seeing a portion of heaven's glory; hold it near and dear to you. Let your knowledge feed your spirit that you may live worthy of the grace bestowed upon you by the One who loves you. Remember that you have not been given this grace only for yourself; it comes for a purpose. Share your faith and knowledge with others, for in that will your Heavenly Father be glorified."

In listening to Revealael, Peter was deeply moved. He was totally amazed that such personal feeling and outright passion would be expressed to him by the angel. It was one thing for Revealael to say that men and angels were both destined for the same glory, but another to see the angel so passionately express himself to a man. Truly, Peter thought, this angel must respect and love him as much, or more, than he had come to respect and love the angel.

What touched Peter more than anything that the angel had said, was the manner in which Revealael had spoken. He obviously loved God more than all else because when he spoke of the Almighty, Peter saw a certain sparkle in his eye and heard a passion in his voice.

Pondering this thought, it dawned upon Peter that he had no doubt noticed exactly that which he was supposed to notice. In fact, as he looked at Revealael, he was sure he could detect the angel looking upon him with an expectation for what he would say next.

It wasn't hard to speak the words Peter knew he must, not after witnessing, at least in some small measure, Revealael's tremendous love of God, and so he requested, "Revealael, please pray for me that I might some day love God as you do. I want that more than anything else."

"I have and I will continue to pray for you, Peter," he revealed. "I have prayed for you continuously since the day you were conceived in your mother's womb."

"You have?"

"Yes, and I will continue to pray for you."

"I feel as though I cannot have enough prayers said for me. I have been so confused," confessed Peter as he again thought back on the past few years.

"I understand," agreed Revealael. "You do not live in an easy time. The battle rages. In a very real sense, this is the age of Satan. For as the Scriptures foretold, in the appropriate time Satan will be loosed from his prison and will come out to deceive the nations.

"Looking at the condition of the world through the wisdom of God clearly shows your age to be the most depraved in the history of the world. Yet, mankind overwhelmingly sees itself as good because it follows the standards of man. Ways that, as you have seen, are actively encouraged by the evil ones. Formulating standards that he can easily follow, man congratulates himself for living such a principled life. How sad it is.

"Indeed, it is exactly as the *Psalm of the Angels* attests:
> The time is short and the end is near,
> but Armageddon, no one knew.

"Even many of those who wish to follow Jesus do not see it because they have been convinced to look for false signs. But, if one will only look to what Jesus said about the end times and not to what others have tried to manufacture from certain Scriptures, they will see that the Battle of Armageddon has been underway for some time."

"You mean we are in the Battle of Armageddon right now?" protested Peter. "I thought that was supposed to be an actual physical war."

"Many have come to expect a preparation for and subsequent physical war to be the meaning of Armageddon. It is not. Do not let those voices fool you. The Great Battle is spiritual. If it were not spiritual, it could not be called the greatest battle of all time. Always remember, as the Scriptures attest, that the greatest battle is not against flesh and blood; it is in the spiritual realm. This is not the only false teaching that is popular in your day concerning the end times.

"Some have come to expect the rapture of the Church to precede a thousand-year period when Christ will rule a material Kingdom on Earth. It will not. The thousand years have ended, and as Jesus said, the Kingdom is in your midst. Remember, time is a creation of the Almighty. To God, a day is as a thousand years and a thousand years as a day. Christ has reigned powerfully for two millennium to those who have accepted His Kingship."

"Will there be a rapture then?" questioned Peter.

"Yes, but the exact day and hour no one can see; only the Father in heaven knows. But there are signs that are given as warnings. The Lord says to always be prepared because that day will be as in the time of Noah. At that time they were eating, drinking, and marrying as though nothing unusual was about to happen. Then, disaster swept them away. Jesus says that it shall be like this at His Second Coming. It is then that He will rapture His Church.

"Normalcy will be the stage for the Lord's coming, not a horrendous physical war. Spending much time looking for unusual signs is not for the Christian. Preparing one's heart and proclaiming the Good News is their calling.

"I will tell you the truth. I do not know the day and hour of His coming, but I do know that there is nothing known to man that now hinders His arrival.

"He who is coming, will come swiftly, like a thief in the night. Therefore be ready, for He is coming at an hour when you least expect. Share this with others. Today is the day of salvation. Today is the acceptable day to do the will of God. Tomorrow may be too late."

"I am not sure what is the will of God," confessed Peter. "How can I really know what God desires for me?"

"One way to know God's will is to closely examine that which you are considering and see if it gives glory to God or does it just glorify you. For example, does it cause you to obey God's Word? If so, then doing it will give glory to God. Would doing it cause you to look good to other people but disobey the fullness of God's Word? If so, then it is not God's will and doing it would only aid the kingdom of darkness.

"Remember, Peter, knowing the will of God involves more than just good logic. No one can know the things of God unless God reveals them. God's grace is necessary.

"No one makes a fool of God! A man reaps from what he sows. To expect God to reveal His will, a person must submit himself and his will to the Almighty. He must be obedient to what God has already revealed to him before he can expect God to further reveal more of His will.

"Never has it been said better than it was by Saint Paul when he proclaimed, 'And be not conformed to this world but be ye transformed by the renewing of your mind, that ye may prove what is the good, and acceptable, and perfect, will of God.'

"Conforming not to the ways of the world but to the ways of God allows the Spirit to transform a person's mind into God's way of thinking. That is what Saint Paul meant when he said that 'I am crucified with Christ: never the less I live; yet not I, but Christ liveth in me.' No one should expect to be thinking in a normal, worldly fashion and be able to understand the will of God.

"Paul also said that 'For the preaching of the cross is to them that perish foolishness; but unto us which are saved it is the power of God.' Surely all who do not follow the Lord of Life are headed for destruction.

"Peter you must help others see the necessity of obeying the will of God. People must come to see what great falsehood is being promoted by those who proclaim that they have the wisdom to change God's Word into what they think He would say to your age.

"God is the same, yesterday, today, and forever. His will does not change. His Word does not change. All who pervert the Word of God by trying to make it accept the sinful lifestyles of your world must be confronted and rebuked. Make them aware that the path they are headed on leads to eternal ruin. Share with them the Good News of forgiveness from sin and new life in Christ Jesus."

"But Revealael," pleaded Peter, "who am I to be calling anyone to repentance?"

"You are a lump of clay in the Potter's hands," encouraged the angel. "It is the Potter who is unique. The Potter will form exactly the sort of vessel He desires if the clay will only remain in His hands.

"God's ways are as high above the ways of man as the heavens are above the earth. It is not good to think that you could, or even should, know all the reasons for God's actions. It is man's part to trust in the Almighty. On this earth it would not be desirable for man to know everything. If all was known and seen, where would there be room for faith?

"Faith is necessary. For without faith, man cannot please God. It is not enough to merely believe in God. Man is called to step out in faith and follow Jesus. Faith is a word of action. Without action there is no faith. Share this with those who call themselves Christian and yet have been too ashamed of the Good News to step out into it."

"You keep telling me to do things, but I'm not sure how you want me to go about doing them," replied Peter, somewhat confused. "Could you be a little more specific?"

"You have already seen and know all that is necessary for you to do the will of the Almighty," answered Revealael. "Trust in God. Pray for guidance and you will receive it, one day at a time.

"It is not good to be given too much all at one time. It is not good to feel too much in control or powerful in your walk with Christ. Saint Paul said, 'In weakness, power reaches perfection.' and 'It is when I am weak that I am strong.' Acknowledging our weakness allows God to work powerfully within us. It is good to realize our need for Him each moment of each day."

"Surely," interjected Peter, "there are people much more capable of serving God in these ways than I am."

"The building up of God's Kingdom is accomplished not by man's cleverness or power, but rather by men following the power of the Spirit. It is God's work and man is His helper. Things are this way so that faith might not rest on the wisdom of men, but on the power of God.

"Peter, only be concerned with following Christ in the best way that you can; God will provide the rest. It is His work. Do not let the job that He calls you to do overwhelm you. He will provide the grace that you need, one day at a time."

Trying to imagine all the angel was asking, Peter confessed, "It is just that sometimes I have felt so alone and helpless."

"Your feelings can be a great help to God's plan," encouraged Revealael. "Believe me, this will make it easier for you to console others and lead them to the rich graces of our God. You have great empathy; so use it for the glory of God.

"You have seen the workings of much evil in the world and you should share your knowledge so that others will understand how the rulers of darkness work. Never forget, though, to share the great glory, power, love, peace, hope, and salvation of our God.

"Evil is a powerful force in the world. It is a force that man can not defeat alone. But, do not forget for a moment that God is infinitely more powerful than evil. Those who submit to the Lord of Life will indeed find the strength to reach everlasting life.

"Yes, Peter, proclaim the reality of what is happening in the world, but never forget to boldly proclaim the fact that He whose Spirit dwells within you is greater than he whose spirit dwells in the world!"

"You make me truly believe that I can do all that you have said," replied Peter with a confidence he had seldom felt. "Revealael, you have helped me so much, how could I ever thank you?"

"You have saved the easiest question for last," answered the wise angel. "Peter, by walking steadfast and rock-solid in the Christian heritage that your name symbolizes you will thank me and, more importantly, the Almighty. Your name means rock, and that is who you must be.

"It is time; I must leave you. I have shown you everything that you needed to know. Remember, what I have shown you is not all that is important, only those things that you needed to see. Use all your knowledge wisely, for the glory of God!"

"I have experienced so much," Peter struggled to say. "I just met you and yet feel like I have known you forever. Will I ever see you again?"

"I cannot say," answered Revealael. "Though we Aurora Angels are constantly at work here on earth, we are seldom called to make ourselves visible. I know only of one other time that I will be seen upon the earth. I will appear one day to a future pope. But, that is a long time coming.

"For you, Peter, know that you are very special to me. I have known and loved you for your entire life. Trust me when I say that I will remain near to you and will surely help you when you call out for help. Never forget that Jesus loves you very much, is near to you, and has given you His Spirit to remain with you to comfort you at all time. You will never be alone.

"Always remember that I will hope and pray unceasingly that we may rejoice together forever in heaven. But for now, I must leave."

"Wait!" pleaded Peter. "Could you let me see one more thing before you leave?"

"What is that?" Revealael asked as if he didn't know.

"I remember that you said it was distracting, but it would cause no harm now would it? I mean, could I once again see you as you really are, in your glory?"

"Yes," he answered without pause, "but only because it is a reflection of the glory of God. Remember that what you will see is only a small reflection of God's glory."

And suddenly the sanctuary was filled with dazzling light. Wave upon wave of multi-colored lights proceeded from Revealael as brilliant walls of color. As the power and glory throbbed around him, Peter was once again forced to acknowledge that this sensitive being, this friend, was a powerful Aurora Angel.

The light became stronger and stronger until Peter could no longer see Revealael's face. Flowing outward, the light passed him bringing overflowing peace and joy upon him. This time it was even more wondrous than when Revealael had first revealed it.

The sanctuary became like a mighty strobe, as the walls of light pulsated and flowed like huge curtains in a breeze. Merging together the waves of light within the light projected themselves in wondrous rainbows of power.

Then, at times the curtains of light would merge together and the whole church would flow like the motion of a rolling sea. Peter found his whole being moving in unison with the light and the compelling emotions that it brought.

Thoroughly in the mystery and majesty of light and love's comfort, Peter swayed until he saw visions of the Lord's Glory within the Aurora. Totally enraptured by the wonders of the Lord, all else in the world around him became as naught. God became all. Perfect harmony in a fullness of peace, joy and love with the perfect Lord.

Then, as quickly as the glory that radiated from the angel appeared, it was gone, but Peter did not know or care. He had fallen into an ecstasy of the Spirit.

AURORA ANGELS

CHAPTER 15

To Tell the Truth

Although desiring to remain within the comfort of the Spirit's rest, Peter slowly regained consciousness of his physical presence in the world. It was not an easy transition for him to return to a world seemingly void of all but a shadowy portion of the glory of God. And yet, the remembrance of glory gradually gave way to his awareness of the reality of the kneeler beneath him and the pew in front of him that supported his head.

After several minutes, the afterglow of glory was gone, and the reality of being back in Saint Alphonsus Church was fully upon him. Peter found himself in the second pew from the front on the right side of the Church, exactly where he had been when first approached by Revealael.

Thoughts of Revealael, the other Aurora Angels, and all the things he had experienced passed through his mind like bolts of lightening.

"Surely they had all been real," he thought as a tinge of anxiety passed through him. "Or was it all a dream? Have I just awoken from a dream? No, it couldn't have been; not something that seemed so real. Or could it? How would I know?"

Peter's thoughts returned to the physical realm around him as he heard the door of the reconciliation room swing open. He glanced at his watch. It was exactly four o'clock. Father Marks had entered the church and was ready to hear confessions. He would have to put off thinking about Revealael and all that had happened until later.

Peter arose and quickly moved toward the confessional. He could feel the adrenalin working within his body as his heart beat faster and he prayed, "Dear Lord, help me to make a good confession. Let this not be like the last time."

His mind reflected back to that time about a year earlier when he had come to the point of knowing he needed to go to confession. Hearing that Father Bob, the pastor of a parish about twenty miles from his home, would hear a private confession, Peter made an appointment to go to him one Saturday.

He had gotten a ride with his oldest sister. When they arrived at the church, he entered the specified room and found that there was no screen to allow the option of anonymity. He had wanted to leave immediately. Since Father Bob was ignoring the Church's mandated setting for confession, Peter was afraid the priest was not obedient to the Church in other matters either.

Not wanting to be rude, he stayed and began his confession, although he personally found that a face-to-face confession to the priest was a distracting feature. He found it all too easy to lose track of his thoughts while looking for responses from the priest. The experiences of confession from his childhood, where a wall with a screened window to speak through had separated priest from penitent, seemed much more effective to him.

In spite of the setting, his confession went fairly well until he started to explain his sorrow for not praying every day as he knew he should have. Suddenly, Father Bob sternly rebuked him for his attitude saying, "Don't do that! We've got too many people who think they should be sitting around praying and feeling good about themselves with a 'holier than Thou' attitude!"

At the time, Peter hadn't known what to say or do. The priest's harsh words had stayed with him for a long time thereafter. He knew Father Bob wasn't right in saying what he did, but still, he found himself hearing those words whenever he would find it a difficult time to pray. And there were many times in his weakened spiritual state that he welcomed an excuse not to be bothered with prayer.

Peter hoped his experience with Father Marks would not be like it had been with Father Bob. He prayed that what he had heard was correct. Several people had told him that Father Marks was a holy and obedient priest who followed all the teachings of the Church, and that was why Peter had come here. There were already enough things that he was confused about; he didn't need to be counseled in any more ways that were in conflict with the Faith.

But now, he had to set his mind upon what he would say when he would begin his confession. He had already gone over it many times. Still, he wanted to make sure he told everything. More than anything else in the world, Peter wanted to be completely prepared to make a fresh start with God.

He entered the reconciliation room, closed the heavy door, and found a four-foot long wall that was built with an opaque, black-screened window within it. Beyond the end of the wall one could go around to a chair, he presumed, and confess to the priest face to face if one desired.

Peter no sooner bent his knees onto the kneeler in front of the window when he heard the soft, deep voice of Father

Marks begin making the Sign of the Cross. He immediately joined him in unison, praying, "In the name of the Father, and of the Son, and of the Holy Spirit. Amen."

"Welcome to the Sacrament of Reconciliation," encouraged Father Marks. "May Almighty God grant you the grace necessary for a good confession."

Peter began, "Father forgive me for I have sinned. It has been nearly seven years since my last good confession and in that time I have committed many sins. At that time I went with my father and mother. That was just shortly before my dad passed away. It was quite a shock. He died unexpectedly of a massive heart attack. He was only sixty years old.

"I've prayed and thought about it a lot and I think that is the basis for a lot of the difficulty that I've had, my father's unexpected death, I mean. It was so hard for me to accept. I couldn't understand why such a good man had to die. It made no sense at all to me.

"I felt like I was being torn apart from the inside out and nothing seemed to ease the pain. Then, every time I looked at my mother she seemed even worse than I did. Seeing her in such pain hurt me as much, or more, than my own sense of loss.

"I tried not to, but I couldn't get my mind off all the things that I would miss doing with my dad. I felt cheated and I wanted to turn my mind to other thoughts but everywhere I turned there was something to remind me of him. For months I couldn't make it through a day without breaking into tears several times. I was really miserable.

"Slowly but steadily my sorrow turned into anger. I felt that Dad's death could have been prevented. It should have been prevented. God could have prevented it but He didn't. I was mad at God. Oh, I knew that it was wrong for me to blame God, and I would try to repress the feelings but they were still alive within me.

"I continued to go to church on Sunday, but it became mostly a hollow action. I probably would have stopped going if it hadn't have been for my mother. I just couldn't add to her grief by arguing with her about God. And so I could never bring myself to speak with her about my being mad at God. And then, when mother became ill, I felt even more alienated from God and blamed Him for her health problem.

"But I feel all that is resolved now. I know God has a plan even if I can't always understand it. My part is to believe in Him. I acted very foolish in trying to hurt God by ignoring Him. All I did was hurt myself and I'm sorry.

"Because of my anger I let other sins creep into my life as well. I began occasionally taking God's name in vain. Oh, not where anyone else could hear me, but I did it just the same. I would say I was sorry, but down inside I was trying to punish God.

"I think that is why it took me so long to go to a parish where I could be helped. At first, I was so confused by the things that started happening at my parish in Riverton that I didn't know what to think or do. So many things were being changed to ways contrary to what I had been taught. And then, when I finally realized what was going on there was not really based on the Catholic faith, and was undoubtedly displeasing to God, I took some sort of pleasure out of being a part of it. I wouldn't have admitted it then, but I think it was sort of revenge against God.

"I wasn't being spiritually fed and I became stagnant. Being there was a trap for me. Although, even when I eventually wanted to, I couldn't seem to find the strength to leave.

"Father, I'm not really sure what was happening to me. All I know is that I felt very empty and far from God over the past few years and I know that it is my fault and I'm sorry.

"There were so many things that I didn't understand. But instead of praying about the situation that I was in and seeking to do God's will I would just try to analyze it by myself. I let Mass become a time to think about what people were doing instead of worshiping God.

"What is even worse is that in the last year or so, when I had begun to seek God and His ways, I failed to seek a true confession or leave a parish that I had come to believe no longer had a valid Mass. Staying in that parish nearly drained me of what faith I had left.

"There were so many things that I was confused about. But even then, I was quite sure that changing the Scripture readings was wrong, and reading secular poems instead of the Scripture readings must have been even worse. But I still kept going there. And I hate to even think of how bad it was for me to go along with singing a popular song to replace part of the Eucharistic prayer when I knew that was wrong.

"I don't mean to sound like I'm blaming others for my sins. It was a very bad situation there, but I knew what was happening and went along with it. It's my fault. I'm responsible for my own sins.

"I am also sorry that on several occasions I participated in their General Absolution Service. Throughout the past years I would from time to time realize that there was a need in my life for reconciliation with God and I would make an attempt to do that without fully examining myself. Instead of going to private confession I would take what seemed to be the easy way and go to their Penance Service.

"They were called Communal Penance Services, but it was always advertised in the church bulletin that general absolution would be offered. A few prayers would be said, and then the priest would absolve everyone's sins. There was no provision at all for private confession.

"I knew better than to think that general absolution should be used like that. I can remember my dad teaching me about the proper administering of the Sacrament of Penance when he was preparing me for my First Penance and First Communion, and what was going on there surely was not right.

"I knew that it was not proper in the Church and I attempted what I considered to be the easy path anyway and I'm sorry now. My heart wasn't really in the right place and that is probably why I felt no different after those services than I did before them.

"I did try to go to private confession about a year ago but I let something the priest said distract me and I ended up not making a good confession. And then, I really felt bad towards him and kept those thoughts in my mind for a long time instead of doing the Christian thing and praying for him.

"Several times over the past few years I let impure thoughts linger in my mind. The time I feel the worst about happened right during Mass. It was during the Presentation of the Gifts at Pentecost about three years ago. Young ladies wearing red body suits danced their way to the altar bringing the gifts and my mind wandered into areas it should not enter.

"Also, over this period of time, I lied several times. At first I did it to protect my mother, at least that's what I told myself. I would think, 'I can't let her know about this or that, it will be too hard for her in the condition she is in.'

Later, I found myself stretching the truth when it actually was more for my benefit than hers. I realize now that there is no such thing as a harmless lie. It just keeps getting worse and worse. I made a big mistake and I'm sorry that I started doing that.

"I'm afraid that one of my biggest problems is that I don't know what to do with my life. I get so confused. I feel like I've just been wasting my time, going round and round without ever getting anywhere. I've been working part time and going to college, but although I'm interested in all the classes I've taken and have gotten good grades, I still have no idea what I want to spend my life working at. Lately, I have prayed for guidance but I haven't found it as of yet. Maybe I just can't recognize it.

"Another problem I have is feeling like I'm different. Much of the time I don't fit in with the people around me. Often I don't even want to fit in with what they are doing, but then I think maybe I am wrong and being judgmental towards them. I see so much in the world that I don't want for myself, and yet I still don't know what I do want. God has given me the gift of life and I feel like I'm wasting it, but I don't know what to do to make my life meaningful.

"Father, for these and all my sins I am truly sorry."

"Thanks be to God for a good confession," responded Father Marks. "Today you have progressed greatly towards the true goal in everyone's life—knowing, loving, and serving God. And that is by no measure an easy task in this world that in so many ways denies the existence of God and the sin that comes from disobedience to His law.

"You have felt quite alone in the world and I would say that that is to be expected for someone who has known God and then been removed from His presence, so to speak, due to sin. I ask you to think and pray about this each day. If after being reconciled with God today you do not feel so alone, then by all means thank the Lord each day for His forgiveness and presence in your life.

"You have gone through a very difficult time with the early death of your father. Try to remember that God understands suffering and death. It appears to you that you have lost your only father to death, and so too God lost His only Son to death. But, as death could not claim the Author of Life, remember that neither can it lay claim to those whom, while sharing in Christ's life, leave the visible realm of this world through the doorway of death.

"God understands and is near to you. No one can see Him and His ways without first being moved by His Spirit. So, know that you have most surely not been alone through your struggle. God loves you and has been at your side.

"Concerning your father, from the way I have heard you speak of him, I would ask you to consider that he is possibly walking closer to you now than he ever could have done in this world. Who is to say that it was not his prayers or service for God that helped bring you to the point in life where you are today? We must simply trust and pray, knowing that God has a plan for our lives and will help us to succeed. He wants very much for us to accomplish His will and provides us with everything we need to do so.

"Just possibly, God's plan for you is such that your father could be more helpful to you after passing from this world into the next. This is part of the great Christian benefit we call the 'Communion of Saints.' We believe that once a person belongs to the Body of Christ that nothing except their own decision can separate them from Him. Not even death can take away a person's life in Christ. This is why Jesus tells us that His followers will never die. And if they are always part of His Body, they will always have a purpose and function in that Body. God doesn't have to work through people but He desires to. He shares His life fully with His children.

"When you feel as though you don't fit in, remember the heavenly multitude of believers around you who also never fit in with the ways of the world. You are most correct in not associating too closely with people who have a rebellious and sinful lifestyle. The command to love one's neighbor never requires one to accept or partake in their sins. Quite the contrary, the Christian is to be a light to the world. The Christian is to illuminate the pathway of salvation to a world lost in the darkness of sin.

"Unfortunately all the members of the Church are not the shinning lights that Christ calls them to be. We must, of course, realize that the Church is made up of sinners trying to find their way to the Father. Still, it can be especially disheartening, and even perilously dangerous to the faithful one's soul, when persons in positions of leadership lead Christ's flock down dangerous paths. I fully understand the dilemma you face in trying to find a parish that teaches in harmony with the true faith of the Church which has been handed down to her from Christ. It is a great problem today.

"Pray for the Church. Pray for the parish where you live. Pray that Almighty God will help you to understand and live His Good News. I wish that I could simply tell you to go back to your home parish and overlook its flaws but I know you are speaking of a serious problem and I cannot do that. I would be most glad to have you join us here at Saint Alphonsus. But, I know that for you to commute from Riverton would be a tremendous burden.

"My advice would be for you to attend Mass at the least offensive parish near your home and pray earnestly for it. I would like to encourage you to read your Bible. Remain immersed in God's Word and the evil ones will be unable to penetrate your life, study diligently the Catechism of the Catholic Church as it will greatly help you in forming your faith, and as often as you can, read of the lives of the Saints, for they will teach you the practical ways of following Jesus through this vale of tears. But above all, pray.

"A person's relationship with God is the most important thing in this world. If one allows himself to drift away from the Lord, then sins of lying and lust will inevitable creep into his life. Continue to center your life on God and everything else will fall into place.

"Pray for God's wisdom. Draw near to God and you will allow Him to reveal His ways to you and His plan for your life. Do not limit Him and He will not limit you. Be open to any vocation He might be calling you into. True happiness in this life can only be found by doing the will of God.

"For your penance I want you to pray *The Passion Novena*. You will find it on the bookrack in the far left corner of the vestibule. Please feel free to take a copy of it with you.

"You may now make your act of contrition."

Peter quickly pulled a small Bible out of his coat pocket and opened it to where he had inserted a bookmark. He began reading the various verses from Psalm fifty that he had highlighted with a colored pencil: "Have mercy on me, O God, according to thy great mercy. And according to the multitude of thy tender mercies blot out my iniquity. Wash me yet more from my iniquity, and cleanse me from my sin. For I know my iniquity, and my sin is always before me. Create a clean heart in me, O God: and renew a right spirit within my bowels. Cast me not away from thy face; and take not thy Holy Spirit from me. Restore unto me the joy of thy salvation, and strengthen me with a perfect spirit. Amen."

Father Marks responded, "God, the Father of mercies, through the death and resurrection of His Son has reconciled the world to Himself and sent the Holy Spirit among us for the forgiveness of sins: through the ministry of the Church may God give you pardon and peace, and I absolve you from your sins, in the name of the Father, and of the Son, and of the Holy Spirit. Amen."

Peter made the Sign of the Cross and echoed, "Amen."

The priest said, "Give thanks to the Lord for He is good."

Peter replied, "His mercy endures forever." Then he added, "Thank you very much for all of your encouragement, Father."

"Your welcome, my son. If it would ever be helpful for you to talk to me outside the confessional, please feel free to contact me."

CHAPTER 16

Prepare a Place

Arising from the kneeler, Peter quickly exited the reconciliation room, thinking that others were waiting to enter. To his surprise, no one else was in the church.

"It's a pity," he thought, "that more people are not here to partake of the Sacrament." That thought did not remain for long. He had no desire to ponder anything discouraging. He felt much too good for that.

It had been such a long time since he had an edifying experience with the Sacrament that he forgot it could feel so good after going to confession. Everything Father Marks said seemed to make sense. "Thanks be to God," he thought, "everything I heard about father being a holy priest was true."

With a warm flood of peace within him he started to go to the pew where he had previously been when he remembered the penance given him, and instead, went out the rear of the church and into the vestibule.

He hadn't noticed it earlier, but looking for it now, he immediately saw the bookrack in the far northeast corner of the vestibule. Before he was halfway there, he could see several copies of *The Passion Novena* on the top shelf.

Picking up one, he gazed intently at its cover for a few moments. Peter's thoughts turned to his dad. His father had loved the Rosary, and this book was a Scriptural rosary meditation centered on the Passion of the Lord. It was also a novena, meaning that it was divided into nine sections that were meant to be prayed over the course of nine days. Peter knew that this was an old practice that went back to the nine days after the Ascension of the Lord when the Church waited and prayed for the promised Holy Spirit. His penance, then, would be accomplished over the course of nine days.

With book in hand he again entered the church. He quickly went to the pew where he had previously been. Genuflecting, he pulled down the kneeler, knelt, and began to pray.

"Thank you Lord for the opportunity you have given me. Help me to always do your will. Please give me the strength and wisdom that I need each day to please you. I see and feel in my heart now that you are the true source of joy. Thank you, Almighty Father, for loving me. Help me to love you more and help me to pray my penance in a manner acceptable to you. In Jesus' name. Amen."

Starting to read the book, he was momentarily mesmerized by its first line, as he felt a wave of emotion surge through him, "With such ease can one take the wide path and drift away from our Lord."

"Yes," he thought, "how true those words are. How strange that they have never moved me as they do now." And then smiling to himself, he mused, "Obviously, it's me. I'm quite sure the words haven't changed on their own."

He smiled broadly as he looked at the author's name that was printed on the front cover. He had seen this book many times and he knew that he would not have to take this copy home with him. He had his own. This was a book his dad had written.

He remembered how as a child his family had often prayed this novena together in the evenings. But then, after his father's death, although he sometimes felt pressured into praying the Rosary with his mother, he just couldn't get his heart into the prayers. That is, until recently.

His mind drifted off into thoughts of his dad and how he had tried to pass on to his children his love of praying the Rosary. Peter still could hear his father say, "There are some people who don't understand the beauty of the Rosary. They need to have us gently explain it to them.

"The Hail Mary is usually the prayer that is the biggest stumbling block. But since Jesus told us to pray for one another, who better to ask to pray for you than His mother? It worked well at the Wedding in Cana."

"Yes," Peter thought as he continued reading the Introduction of *The Passion Novena*, "Dad had a way of putting things into perspective. Like this last line 'May we, with the Blessed Virgin's help, come to more clearly see our Lord's way to the Father.' That is what the Rosary is all about."

Looking up at the crucifix hanging on the wall above the altar, Peter prayed, "Lord please help me to concentrate on praying this meditation of your passion. Let it be for your glory and my edification." Then he began his penance, "In the name of the Father, and of the Son, and of the Holy Spirit. Amen."

Time passed quickly. Peter's prayer had been answered as he meditated upon the prayers and Scripture verses with a concentration he had seldom experienced. Before long, he completed his first day of penance and his mind again reflected upon what he had experienced with the angel.

"No way was there enough time for me to fall asleep and dream," he thought to himself. "It all must have really happened. There was only fifteen minutes between the time when I began first praying in the church and when confession started. Revealael must have brought me back here to the exact time when he first announced his presence. There just wasn't enough time for me to have fallen asleep and have dreamed all that, was there?"

Trying to piece it all together, Peter's thoughts drifted off to some of the wonders that he had experienced and some of the things that he now knew which he surely did not know previously. "Definitely," he thought, "I could not know the things that I now know from just an ordinary dream. Whatever happened, it was powerful and very special."

Hearing the church's massive doors swing open and the footsteps of people entering for Mass, his thoughts were brought back to his physical presence in the pew. Soon those footsteps were followed by more, and in a few minutes the church was nearly full.

Peter was impressed that the vast majority of parishioners entered quietly and began to pray in preparation for Mass. It had been a long time since he had been in church and not heard a constant buzz of voices before Mass. Here, a person could actually enter and concentrate on prayer. How refreshing, indeed, was the atmosphere of reverence at Saint Alphonsus.

Shortly, the entrance song was announced and the congregation rose to greet Father Marks. The organ music pouring forth into the church reminded him of some of the music his mother had on tape. "It's too bad mother couldn't have been here," he thought while saying a short prayer for her recovery.

Father Marks entered, greeted the assembly, prayed the opening prayers, the Gloria was sung, and the lector proclaimed the readings from the Word of God. Peter followed along with the readings in the misalette, a habit he had grown accustomed to since, for one reason or another, it was so often difficult to recognize every word that was spoken. He also remembered being taught at a very small age that the more senses a person used in reading, the greater their retention of the material. So, Peter liked to see as well as hear the readings.

But, Father Marks began reading the Gospel with such clarity that Peter lowered his misalette down to his side and let his eyes give the priest their full attention.

It was then that Peter noticed something marvelous had happened. Father Marks was off to the left of Peter, at an angle where Peter would normally have to turn his head far to the left beyond what was normal in order to see clearly with his right eye, since he could not see much from the center of his left eye. Amazingly, Peter did not have to turn his head. His left eye was working perfectly!

Those around him must have thought him a little strange, but Peter never gave that a thought. He dropped his misalette, quickly placing a hand over his right eye. Yes, he was seeing perfectly from his left eye. "Praise God!" he said softly. "It's a miracle. I can see."

Several times he blinked his eyes, looked in different directions, and held his hand over his right eye. The results were consistently the same—the vision in his left eye was perfect. There was no longer any sight missing.

Peter wanted to shout it out to everyone there. In fact, he began to feel a little guilty that he was not sharing the power of God with everyone else gathered there, but Father was right in the middle of reading the Gospel now. Besides, where would he start? His healing could have happened anytime, but he knew when it had. There was no doubt in his mind. He was healed when Jesus had put His hands upon his head. How could he explain that in a few words?

When the Lord touched him, he had felt a wonderful power flow through him. Revealael had made a point of saying that they were actually in the past. Now, Peter knew it for sure. He had physically encountered the Lord Jesus and had been healed by His touch.

Excitedly, he whispered to himself, "Everything I remember experiencing with Revealael really did happen. This proves it. Praise be to God!"

Then the seriousness of it all hit him as he thought over and over, "Now what do I do?"

As Father Marks finished the Gospel, Peter silently prayed, "Dear Jesus, thank you for all that you have done for me this day. Thank you for healing my vision. Even more importantly, thank you for forgiving my sins and healing my soul through your Sacrament. And thank you for all that has been revealed to me this day by your servant, Revealael. May I, through your grace, come to do all that you expect of me. Strengthen me through this Holy Mass to better know, love, and serve you."

Peter tried to keep his thoughts on the homily and prayers of the Mass, but it was difficult. No matter how he tried, he couldn't stop thinking of his healing, Revealael, and, above all, the visions of the glory of God.

It seemed that in no time at all, Father Marks was giving the final blessing. Peter couldn't ever remember a Mass passing by so quickly, but when he looked at his watch he found that Mass had only seemed short; it was now 6:38. He would have to hurry to get back to the bus station by 7:30.

Peter quickly departed Saint Alphonsus Church. He never thought of asking someone for a ride. He had only God on his mind, and the haste necessary to make his bus on time. If anyone had been around to see him marching down the frozen sidewalk they surely would have thought he was practicing for some power-walking competition in the winter Olympics.

The part of Glory Falls that he was traveling through looked even more desolate on a bitter, cold night than it had during the afternoon. Many a man would have avoided walking here for fear of assault, but that never crossed Peter's mind; he had more important things to think about.

He glanced up at the temperature that was displayed above a bank across the street and realized just how cold he was. It read minus twenty-three degrees. Pulling his stocking cap down to better cover ears that were beginning to feel a little stiff and tingly, he let his hands pass down for a moment and rest over his mouth and nose, letting his breath bring them warmth.

The cold seemed to travel through every inch of him, from his head, through his spine, and right down to the tips of his toes. It reminded him of the awful time when he was five years old and had stepped into a hole while ice fishing. Then, his dad had been there to rescue him from the ice-cold lake. How Peter wished that he was here to help him now.

Quickly his thoughts returned to his destination, as the display on the bank switched from temperature to time. He would have to hurry. Now he wished he had more seriously considered asking one of his brothers or sisters to bring him here. They would not have refused, but, still, he hated to impose on them since they had already done so much for him.

"Oh, for the days when everyone owned a car," he thought, as he picked up his pace, and the sound of his shoes striking the frozen walk took on a new, faster rhythm. It would really have been nice to be able to take a taxi to the bus station, but he spent nearly everything he had on the bus fare.

Money was scarce, and almost all he made from working thirty hours or so a week at the car wash went to pay for tuition at the university. Living with his mother, just outside of Riverton, was fortunate for him; he could walk to nearly every place he needed to go. With the economy the way it was, he considered himself fortunate to be able to ride the bus for the fifty miles from Riverton to Glory Falls.

Life definitely had not been easy these past few years, especially since his mother became sick. The strain of raising four teenagers by herself surely was considerable. Although there really were five through part of those years, since Peter's oldest brother was living at home until two years ago. Mother had pretty much treated him the same as the other children even though he was then nearly thirty years old.

Peter always looked up to his oldest brother, who had been very good to him and honestly tried hard to provide him with a father image. That was not an easy task, especially for someone who was only ten years older than Peter. The youngest son had grown to appreciate very much the oldest son's diligent efforts, though, and admired him greatly for them all.

Remembering how his dad always said to warm up by flapping your arms, he began to vigorously swing his arms. For the first time since leaving the church, Peter became conscious of the fact that there might be someone else nearby and he began to look around. "There's nobody in sight," he thought, "good thing, because if anyone saw me they surely would think I'm crazy. But, Dad was right; it does help."

"Yes," he reflected, while feeling a tear form in his eye, "Dad taught me a lot about life. I wish he were here to help me now." But his dad wasn't there to help. Peter knew he must act like an adult and make his own decisions.

"How could things have gotten this bad?" he wondered. "Dad sure would have been shocked to see that a person would have to travel fifty miles to go to the Sacrament of Reconciliation. On second thought, maybe he wouldn't have been too surprised." Peter thought back to his youth and all those hours he had spent with his dad discussing religion, trying to hear the words which his father would have spoken at a time like this. It was hard, partially because it seemed in many ways like such a long time ago and partially because he usually avoided thinking about his dad. Thinking about his dad just ended up making him hurt inside.

The family was always close. His mother and dad had home-schooled their children. All that time they spent working together was a tremendous facilitator for bonding the family together, but losing his dad, however, had disrupted the family greatly. Things were much different than what they used to be. Then, their home was full of children and laughter, but now just Peter and his sick mother were all who occupied that big house.

"Maybe Father Marks was right about dad helping me in ways I never realized," he murmured to himself as he began to think about some of the things his father had written. Peter knew that more than anything else, what his dad had written in his books had changed his attitude.

They were presently fresh in his mind, but until this last year Peter had kept the copy of each tucked away into the top dresser drawer in his room where he wouldn't see them. They always meant a lot to him because they all contained a note signed by his dad. Still, Peter hadn't read any of them since his father's death; he just couldn't bring himself to do it. That is, until last year. Since then, he couldn't put them out of his mind.

Over the course of the last year it seemed to Peter like a part of his father was alive and back with him again. One of the books his dad had written was about the struggles he encountered as a young man coming to a personal relationship with Jesus. It was especially relevant to Peter because at that time his dad had been just about the same age as Peter was now.

The change in Peter's heart really began after reading, with an adult perspective, how his father had struggled to come to the Lord and the resulting change that Jesus made in his life. In honestly looking at himself, Peter saw that faith had brought a peace and joy to his dad's life that he had never known, and he wanted that for himself.

Making it into the warmth of the bus station he was reminded of the warmth this day had brought to his heart. He felt so much better now that he had finally been reconciled with God. He had wanted the faith of his father and today it felt alive within him. The cold or nothing else could take that away.

With all the day's events going through his mind, the bus ride home went so fast that before he knew it he was back in Riverton walking through the front door of the only home he had ever known. His mother, concerned about him being out for so long on such a cold day, was waiting up for him.

Prepare a Place

When he sat down next to here and told all that had happened to him, her concern was turned to a joy he had not seen in her since before his father's death. Her words would remain deep within him.

"Peter, dear," she said, "I am just so happy for you. And your sight... praise be to God! You've been healed. So many blessings, all in one day. I don't know what to rejoice in first."

Then, drawing him near to her, she hugged him warmly as she said, "I always knew that something very special was awaiting you in life. Now you must pray and wait for the Spirit's guidance."

AURORA ANGELS

CHAPTER 17

A Call Through Fire

Days quickly turned into weeks as Peter followed Father Mark's advice about discerning the will of God. He canceled his classes for the new term at the University and devoted his time to prayer, study, and his mother. Praying the Rosary, studying the Bible, and reading the classic works of the Saints and Doctors of the Church became his daily habit.

On the days when there was morning Mass he would rise early and walk the two miles across town to Blessed Virgin Parish. It was hard, especially after seeing the things that had been revealed to him, but he prayed earnestly and exerted no small effort in keeping his mind on God rather than on Father Moe's antics during Mass. And God greatly blessed him.

On the days when there was no Mass, Peter would go to the church where he would pray alone for an hour or so. Although he missed receiving the Lord in the Eucharist, those were especially insightful times for him. In the quietness he could best hear the voice of God.

Occasionally he would let his mind wander to imagine how things might be if someone like Father Strong or

Bishop LaRock were there at Blessed Virgin Church. Then one morning after he had prayed, when he was leaving, he found a small card lying on the vestibule floor. He picked it up and immediately knew its message was for him. It said, "Better to light one candle, than to curse the darkness."

It was a saying Peter had heard before, but this time it was especially meaningful. This time he knew in his heart that it was directed straight at him. Finally, after nearly three months of searching, he was sure of what he must do.

That afternoon, Peter called Father Marks and told him that he felt called to holy orders. The good priest said he would be more than happy to speak with Peter and counsel him. So, the next day found Peter journeying to Saint Alphonsus Church in Glory Falls.

Peter explained everything to Father Marks. That afternoon both men were greatly blessed by the encounter and sharing in the glory of God. Father Marks had a welcome surprise for Peter. He confirmed Peter's calling to the priesthood. He revealed that on the day Peter had first come there to confession, the Spirit had revealed to him that the young man who was about to enter the confessional had a priestly calling. So over the past few weeks Father Marks had been investigating to see which seminaries might have openings.

He had found that there were many seminaries with openings, but of those he judged to be faithful to the Catholic Tradition all were filled. There was one possible exception, Trinity Seminary, which was located about 250 miles southwest of Glory Falls. It had always been a faithfully orthodox seminary, but lately Father had heard a few discouraging things, and now he was not sure about it. He advised Peter that if he wanted to go there and see for himself, then an interview would be arranged.

Peter was eager to go, and so Father Marks made an appointment for him to be interviewed. Before leaving for home, Father heard his confession and Peter departed feeling a great sense of joy in now having a confidence in what the purpose and direction of his life should be.

Peter was overjoyed in his new friend. It was the first time in his life that he personally knew a priest he could look up to. Truly, Father Marks was a man content in calling Jesus his Lord and in his vocation; he was a fine example of what being a priest should be.

A warm March day one week later found Peter on a bus pulling into the small town of Naples that was home to Trinity Seminary. It had been an all-day trip, but one he had been anxious to make. Thinking of his calling and all that lie ahead of him made the hours fly by. And now, he could see the large seminary building through the bus window, only a short walk from the bus stop.

The sun was already low in the west by the time he headed down the sidewalk. Upon arriving, he rang the doorbell and was greeted by a large, middle-aged lady who was dressed in jeans and a sweatshirt. Her graying brown hair was on top of her head in a bun, and he immediately noticed the excessive makeup on her face. Peter thought she was probably the housekeeper; but he was wrong.

"Can I help you?" she said, authoritatively.

"Yes," he answered, "I'm Peter York, and I am here for an interview."

"Come in," she returned, "we have been expecting you. I'm Sister Ann. Have you had anything to eat for your supper?"

"Yes I have, thank you," he replied, thinking it strange for a sister not to be wearing her religious habit if this was a truly orthodox Catholic seminary.

"I ate a short while ago when the bus made its stop back in that little town of Lewiston."

"Well then, follow me," said Sister Ann, "and I will show you to your room. You must be tired from your trip. We will send someone to wake you in the morning, and then your interview will be after breakfast."

"Will you be having an evening prayer service that I could participate in?" questioned Peter.

"No, we aren't having any communal prayers during this time of the year," answered sister.

Seeking to better understand the spiritual life there at the seminary Peter inquired, "Will you be having prayers in the morning?"

"No. We only have communal prayers during Lent and Advent," she replied curtly as though she already grew tired of his questions.

Even though he felt like he was asking all the wrong questions, Peter, didn't want to miss receiving the Eucharist the following day and so he asked, "What time is Mass tomorrow morning?"

"We only have Mass on Fridays," she answered in a slow deliberate manner as if he was hard of hearing. "But anytime you want to you can go to our chapel. It is right down the hall from your room, around the first corner to the second door on the left."

Sister Ann left him at his room. Peter unpacked his traveling bag, washed up, and decided to go to the chapel to pray.

Upon entering the chapel, he was disheartened to find that the Blessed Sacrament was not reserved there. The chapel was basically a bare room with a dozen chairs in a circle around a simple wooden table. Except for a small, six-inch high cross standing on the table and a banner on the wall that said, "We are Church," the room was empty. There wasn't a Bible or a prayer book to be found.

Peter knelt upon the floor for a few minutes and prayed, but he couldn't quite get his heart into it so he went back to his room where he read from his Bible and used it to meditate and pray.

After a long night of tossing, turning, and trying to discern what he had already witnessed at Trinity Seminary, morning came. There was a knock at the door and a male voice announced that it was time to get up, as breakfast would be ready in half an hour. Peter welcomed the thought of breakfast, but he had been up for nearly two hours. Not being able to sleep any longer, he had shaved, showered, prayed the Rosary, and spent the better portion of an hour meditating upon The Fifth Part of Saint Francis de Sales' *Introduction to the Devout Life*, which is an exercise on renewing one's soul in the Christian life.

Peter went down to breakfast and met two seminarians, Father Charlie, and Mrs. Hull, an elderly lady who prepared a hearty breakfast. Peter had waited for everyone to be served their food, thinking there would be a common blessing, but when the others just began to eat, Peter bowed his head and prayed by himself.

In conversation, he learned that Father Charlie was the rector of the seminary, and so Peter assumed that his interview would be with him; but he was wrong again. Soon, Sister Ann, who was dressed nearly identical to the previous day, entered and sat down. When he had finished his meal, she led him to a nearby office where she had him sit across from her at a large wooden desk.

"I have a number of questions to ask you, Peter," she said. "They are based on a psychological approach that we have been using for some time to indicate the overall suitability that prospective candidates would have if ordained. Please answer the questions with what first comes to mind. It is your natural tendencies that we are concerned with, and too much reflection hinders the process. Any questions before we begin?"

"No, ma'am," answered Peter, slightly mystified at the direction towards basic instincts that the interview seemed to be taking.

"And please, just call me Ann," requested the sister. "I am no different than you. Now, let's get started.

"First of all, I want you to consider a situation. You are out on the ocean in a small boat fishing with three other people. One person is paralyzed from the shoulders down and in a wheel chair. Another has been diagnosed with bone cancer and has been given only six months to live. The third is a newly retired person in their mid-fifties who is in good health.

"A storm quickly and unexpectedly comes up, capsizes the boat, and it begins to sink. Only one small, three-man, inflatable life raft can be found. Who do you attempt to convince to remain off of the raft?"

"I would put the others on the raft and attempt to stay afloat in the water," answered Peter.

"Why would you do that? You would certainly drown! Why, as a healthy young man, would you sacrifice yourself?" asked Ann sternly.

"Well, I have faith in the Lord," replied Peter, "and I don't know about the others, maybe they need more time upon this earth."

"In other words, you feel yourself to be superior to other people?" questioned sister.

"No, not at all," pleaded Peter, surprised at her reply. "But, I know that it is necessary to die in God's grace. I have an understanding about where my relationship with God is at any particular time in my life, but I don't know about other people."

"So, you think that what you have experienced in your life is the only way for other people to travel life's journey?" she questioned. "What of those who have never heard of Christ?"

"I would not say that it is impossible for people to somehow come to God without hearing and following the Gospel. I know that all things are possible for God, but I think that it would be extremely difficult. I know that no one can come to the Father except through the graces flowing from the works of Jesus, and that He formed a Church and gave it the mission of preaching His Good News to all the peoples of the world for the salvation of souls."

Forcefully she responded, "You don't think that as a young healthy person you would be able to do much more good in the world during your lifetime?"

"I don't think that I should ever do what I consider a bad thing with the hope that good may come from it," answered Peter.

"Oh, then you believe that there are hard and fast absolute truths, things that are always true no matter what the circumstances and intentions," questioned Ann sarcastically.

"Well, yes," replied Peter, "I most certainly do believe that there are objective truths."

"Interesting," mused Sister Ann. "So tell me, do you think that a priest should confront parishioners that he thinks are living in sin and correct them? For example, a man and a woman are living together and are, for whatever reason, not married. They both come to Mass regularly and receive communion. Do you think the priest should approach them and challenge their lifestyle?"

"I think that would be appropriate, even a responsibility of the priest. Of course, it should be done in a confidential manner, without causing them embarrassment," answered Peter.

She quickly blurted, "Don't you think that is being a little judgmental?"

"I think we need to be very careful in correcting other people, but still that is what the Lord calls us to do," replied Peter. "I think that is especially true here in your analogy. You are speaking about the people's pastor. It is not the sin that we are called to not judge, it is the person. I have always been taught to love the person, but to hate the sin. I think there is a big difference."

"I see," said Ann. "Let's move on to another hypothetical situation. What would you do if, as the pastor of a parish, you were questioned by one of your parishioners about holding a weekly Mass for gays?"

"I would be opposed to treating them as a special group, unless there was some overriding circumstance, which I cannot now foresee," answered Peter. "Would this be a group who were attempting to be chaste or one that simply wanted a special Mass of their own, sort of legitimatising their lifestyle?"

"Would that matter?" she asked.

"I would certainly think so. I would want to help them overcome their problem, not encourage it," he replied.

"Oh!" continued Ann sharply. "Well then, another question: Do you think that you would have any problem working side by side with a woman priest?"

"Yes," answered Peter slowly, becoming more than a little disgusted by the questions being asked. "If that were to happen I would know that something very terrible had indeed occured."

"Why? What do you mean?" demanded Sister Ann. Stiffening in her chair, she scowled across the table at him.

"The Holy Father has, in unison with Church Tradition, declared that the ordination of women cannot happen. Even the Pope does not have the authority to change that!" Peter answered forcefully.

"Oh really," responded Ann, "that's interesting." Then smiling as her voice turned sweet, said, "Well, I think we have gone through enough questions to conclude this interview. Wait here and I will be back shortly, after reviewing our interview with Charlie."

Sister Ann quickly left the room, but in less than a quarter of an hour she returned. Entering the room, she silently stood by her chair for a moment with a look that suggested to Peter that she would thoroughly enjoy what was about to be said.

"I am sorry, but Father Charlie agrees totally with me in your unsuitability as a candidate for the priesthood. It is necessary for a priest, above all else, to be open-minded and flexible, and you do not have either quality. For your own good we would advise you to find a career in life where it is not required of you to personally interact with other people. We do thank you for thinking of our seminary and wish you the very best in life."

And with that she abruptly left Peter to find his way out. Peter felt sick over the experience, but was glad to be leaving this place where he knew, beyond a shadow of a doubt, that he did not belong.

Over and over within his mind on the way home Peter relived all that had happened to him over the past few months. He was sure of his calling to the priesthood. Still, it was disturbing for him to have been questioned in such an unchristian way. And the fact that he would probably have to wait at least a year before he could enter a good seminary was somewhat disappointing to him.

Reassuring to him, though, was Father Marks' confidence in his call. Father Marks was, indeed, a good priest and friend. "That's it," he thought, "I will stop and see Father Marks on the way home. I have to travel right through Glory Falls anyway."

So in a few hours Peter found himself being let into the Saint Alphonsus rectory by Father Marks.

"It is so good to see you," greeted the good priest. "How did your interview go?"

"Not well," answered Peter, as he began to tell him everything.

"Oh, Peter, I am so sorry," replied the priest, after hearing all that had transpired. "I never would have believed that Trinity Seminary would have fallen so far from the faith. What seems to be their acceptance of subjective morality is especially disappointing.

"Even after all that has happened around me over the past few years, I still find such deviations from authentic, Catholic teaching hard to believe. God must have wanted you to have that experience, so use it to grow in your Christian faith. Remember that the Lord works in mysterious ways.

"God often provides exactly what we need just when we think we have completely run out of possibilities. For example, this very morning I received word from a retired priest, who was one of my professors in seminary, of a possible opening at a excellent seminary that I positively know for a fact, is one of the finest English-speaking seminaries in the world.

"I called the rector, who is an old friend. After I told him about you he said that he would accept your entrance into his seminary based on my judgment of your qualification."

"That is wonderful!" exclaimed Peter excitedly. "What seminary is it?"

"The name of the seminary is 'Holy Angels,' but it does have one slight drawback, it is quite some distance away. Although, that actually could be very advantageous, considering the present situation of the Church here."

"Where is it?" questioned Peter anxiously.

With a noticeable reservation Father Marks answered, "Holy Angels Seminary is located about eighty miles northeast of London, England."

AURORA ANGELS

CHAPTER 18

Orders

The smell of the salt air and the gentle sea breeze were like a tonic to him every time he walked along the seashore. Peter loved England, and these early-morning walks he had grown accustomed to were especially dear to him.

With the thin fog rising up from the warmth of the first light of day, he could not help but marvel at the scene around him. In every direction he saw beauty.

"Surely," he thought, "it was no wonder that so many great poets, playwrights, and others of creative talent had come from this land. This beautiful island of green meadows and tree covered hills, surrounded by the majestic sea, vividly stands as a proclamation of the glory of God."

How fortunate Peter felt to have been able to come here to Holy Angels Seminary. Situated in the country on a cliff overlooking the sea with its huge old stone walls, it had the charm that made it look like something one might find on the pages of a children's fairy tale.

All he had to do was follow the ancient path that twisted its way down the cliff and he was able to be soothed and regenerated by the action of the sea. He loved the sound of the waves caressing the shore.

Maybe it was in Peter York's blood to love this land. After all, as his surname attested, Peter's ancestors had no doubt roamed this land and the waters surrounding her. And then, maybe it was because he felt so good about what he had been doing with his life over the past three years. Seeing the marvelous hand of the Creator in the world around him, Peter most likely would have loved the countryside no matter where he would have been. Regardless of the reason, he was very happy in England.

More importantly, he had been doing excellent work at the seminary. The solid education he had received through his home-schooling, especially the Greek and Latin he began studying in sixth grade, combined with his prior university work, had made it possible for him to minimize greatly his seminary time. After only three years here at Holy Angels, he was about to be granted degrees in Scripture, Theology, and Cannon Law.

People had always considered Peter to be extremely intelligent, although he had never fully applied himself to study before coming to Holy Angels. Oh, he pulled A's in college, all right, but without using his potential. Now it was completely different.

For the first time in his life Peter knew what he wanted and he was determined to give it every effort. No matter what Peter studied he felt as though he was learning more about the Lord of Creation. Through it all, he would often think of Revealael and what the angel had shown him; then Peter would be driven to work that much harder.

Peter felt fulfillment for the first time of his life. He had even grown to accept his father's death, and, in fact, often thought of his dad and received pleasure from doing so. The one thing that he felt bad about was being away from his mother, but even that feeling had diminished. She

Orders

received great pleasure in knowing that Peter was studying for the priesthood. At least that is what she often expressed to him in her letters.

And then, Peter would tell himself, "Mother is not alone. She has two other sons and two daughters who are very responsible and all live within a fifteen-minute drive from her. Mother is well taken care of."

Still, Peter had faithfully written to his mother for the past three years, just as he told her he would do. When he left home, he promised to write to her every other day and pray the Rosary for her intention every day. That had pleased her very much.

Peter finished his morning walk down the beach and had just progressed up the winding path to the top of the cliff when he noticed someone running toward him. It was Jonathan, a fellow seminarian.

"Peter!" came a shout from the young man running towards him, as though Peter could miss seeing his bulky six-foot four-inch frame in motion no more than two-hundred feet from him. Then, when Jonathan was nearly upon Peter, he struggled to deliver his message while gasping for air, "Peter, Father Crowley sent me to fetch you. He needs to see you in his office right away."

"Did he say why he wanted to see me?" questioned Peter.

"No!" answered Jonathan. "Only for me to get you."

Peter couldn't imagine why Father Crowley, the seminary rector, would want to see him so urgently, but in any case, he thanked Jonathan and began jogging back to the seminary.

In Peter's estimation, Father Crowley was the perfect seminary rector, if ever there was one. Peter had no trouble seeing why Father Crowley and Father Marks were good

203

friends; they were so much alike. Both took their calling to the priesthood very seriously. It was obvious that both considered living a holy lifestyle not as something optional for a Christian, especially one called to holy orders.

When he first came to Holy Angels, Peter chose Father Crowley as his confessor and spiritual advisor and could claim from experience his likeness to Father Marks in the confessional. Both not only helped him greatly, but also had given him wonderful examples of how a priest could powerfully use the sacrament of reconciliation to help people become more Christ-like.

It took Peter but a few minutes to make his way to the familiar door of Father Crowley's office. After a couple of sharp knocks, the priest appeared. Something about him seemed different to Peter. The rector's snow white hair and bright blue eyes were the same, but the familiar smile was gone. Standing in the doorway, he looked serious, in a way that Peter had not seen before.

"Peter, please come in and have a seat," welcomed Father Crowley slowly motioning towards a big wooden chair. Then, as Peter sat down, Father Crowley pulled another chair directly over in front of him and sat down. For a few moments, the priest sat motionless.

"You wanted to see me about something?" Peter questioned, not knowing if Father Crowley was waiting for him to speak first.

"Yes, Peter," began the priest, "I did. I received a telephone call this morning from Father Marks. I am afraid he had some bad news; your mother passed away last night."

"Mother gone?" responded Peter in a choked voice. "I didn't realize she was that sick. What happened?"

"Well, from what we know, she seemed to have passed on very peacefully last evening. When your youngest sister stopped by her house she found your mother in her rocking chair. They don't know for sure, but think she had a heart attack. She had obviously been praying the Rosary at the time of her death because her Rosary was still in one hand and one of your father's Scriptural Rosary books in the other."

"That sounds like mother," said Peter trying to hold back the tears. "She would pray the Rosary every morning and evening. I have expected this for a long time; but still, I dreaded the thought. I wish I could have been there with her."

"You will be pleased to know that Father Marks was with her yesterday afternoon," said Father Crowley, trying to comfort him. "He heard her confession and gave her Communion. As you no doubt know, Father Marks had been stopping to visit your mother once a month, on the way north to visit his aging aunt.

"He also said to tell you not to worry about any of the funeral arrangements; your mother had taken care of everything. Her funeral Mass will be at Saint Alphonsus Church with Father Marks presiding on the day after tomorrow."

Father Crowley himself drove Peter down to Heathrow. Peter always loved the view when approaching London on his previous visits there, but on that day the thought of the view never crossed his mind.

The traffic was bad on the way to the airport, and then after getting there he had to wait through several delays. It seemed such a long time before he actually got into the air and was headed home.

Once home, Peter was quite surprised to hear how hard the past nine months since he last been home to visit had taken their toll on his mother. She never let on to him how much her health had been failing. In fact, she went so far as to give the other children strict orders not to mention the condition of her health to Peter. She wanted nothing to interfere with his studies. "That was mother all right," thought Peter after he had heard of it. "She was always concerned with not worrying me."

Peter would dearly miss her. Yet, looking upon her lifeless, thin corpse, and seeing how much she obviously suffered these past months from her cancer made it easier for him to let her go.

Peter could not believe how fast the time went. Before he knew it, the week vanished. It was an enlightening time, too. He never realized how enthused his brothers and sisters were at the prospects of him becoming a priest, nor had he understood the magnitude of joy that his call made in his mother's life, until he heard it proclaimed from all his family. It was so much easier for him to prepare to leave for the seminary when he knew he had the prayers and support of his whole family.

Then, before he found adequate time to assimilate all that had happened, he was back on a plane about to land in England. When Peter disembarked the plane and entered the terminal at Heathrow, he found Jonathan waiting to take him from the airport back to Holy Angels. Surprisingly, the seminarian had nearly the same message for Peter as when they last met.

When they reached the seminary, Peter went directly to Father Crowley's office. "Good to see you back with us," welcomed the priest along with a firm handshake. "I trust you had a safe trip?"

"Yes, Father, I did." replied Peter. "It was very good to see my brothers and sisters again. It was not as difficult as I imagined over the years that it would be to accept the

Lord's will concerning my mother. I am sure her faith will not be disappointed."

"I wish I could have known her," offered Father Crowley. "From everything I have heard, she was truly a fine Christian woman, a real example to her family and all those around her.

"I, of course, wanted to welcome you back, but the reason I called you here, so soon upon your arrival, is of a different nature. I received a telephone call from Cardinal Bancoli at the Vatican while you were in America. I should tell you that it was not a totally unexpected conversation.

"As you have probably heard, they have recently been training a few men from outside their order. I petitioned the cardinal to accept you into the Angelicum for your last two years of training. He called to inform me that you have been chosen."

"I don't know what to say," said Peter stumbling over his words. "I never dreamed of being selected to go there."

"Believe me, I hate to see you leave us," explained the priest with a strained voice, "but, I think that it is better for the Church that you do."

"What do you mean, Father?" interrupted Peter.

"I have been rector at this seminary for over thirty-five years, and I have never seen a man with a calling so obviously strong as the one that you have to the priesthood. Your deep faith, understanding of Christianity, and ability to retain a wide spectrum of knowledge in the classroom setting, along with the heartfelt compassion that I have seen flow freely from you to others are qualities that must be encouraged to grow to their fullest potential for the good of the Church."

In his heart Peter resisted leaving Holy Angels, but he knew that Father Crowley was helping him to make the best decision. Studying at the Angelicum in Rome would offer him the most comprehensive education possible.

"Yes," he thought, "that would surely give me a greater feel for the universal Church; there would be people there from every nation in the world. Also, all the heritage of the Church that lies within the Vatican would be at my disposal. This is truly a providential opportunity."

And so, once again, Peter left a land and people that he loved behind him, and he journeyed to the Eternal City. Once there, he drank in deeply from the fountains of its vast treasury. Within the walls that marked Vatican City and throughout Rome he intensely studied the ancient heritage of Christianity.

His achievement rose to an even higher level than that which he had enjoyed at Holy Angels. Now, his rest came not from the long walks upon the seashore, but through reliving the history of each and every building and artifact of Christian significance that he came into contact with. Peter was literally in love with Rome.

Then one day, a somber reality descended upon the Church. Father Gaudini, rector of the Angelicum, personally made the rounds announcing the most sorrowful event that had happened.

"I am sorry to inform you," he began, "but today it has been formally announced by several cardinals and bishops of the Church in the United States of America, that they will no longer follow any directives from the Holy See. They have formed an independent national assembly and will operate under the name American Catholic Church. The Vatican has issued a statement asking all Catholics to earnestly pray for our now-separated brethren and for a speedy resolution and healing of the problems that brought about this painful situation.

"The Holy Father personally called upon all of the faithful to be aware of this schism and self-imposed excommunication. He does not want anyone to unwittingly join in these rebellious actions and be drawn away from the faith of our Lord Jesus Christ."

Peter could feel his heart drop in his chest. He had known this was a real possibility, but still, had hoped, prayed, and thought that conversion would take place before schism. He was wrong.

He thought of his brothers and sisters, and Father Marks. How were they taking all of this? "Surely," he thought, "the diocese of Glory Falls would be with those forming the American Church."

Then, he realized that he most probably knew the answers to his questions. Revealael had shown them to him. He wished Revealael were here to give him more direction now, and he remembered the angel telling him not to worry about the future, but to look toward Jesus.

"Just one day at a time," is what Revealael had said. "God will give you the grace you need at the time and day that you need it." And Peter bowed his head and ask the angel to join him as he prayed for the grace to make it through the day.

The days and weeks passed on rapidly. About three months later, Peter was called into Father Gaudini's office. He began by announcing something Peter had worked hard to hear.

The good father said, "Peter, I have been very pleased to have you here at the Angelicum; your work has been performed most excellently. This fact has not gone unnoticed by many others as well. We all are more than confident of your preparation and readiness for ordination to the diaconate, and because of the present situation within your home diocese, we would like that to take place here, in Rome, at the Basilica of Mary Major."

"The Pope's Church?" questioned Peter quite surprised.

"Yes," answered Father Gaudini. "The Holy Father wants us to do everything possible to make you seminarians from the United States know, understand, and feel a part of the heart of the Church. Also, I think you will be pleased to know that the Cardinal Prefect of the Doctrine of the Faith will be administering the Sacrament to you."

"Cardinal Kullinzer, himself?" Peter blurted out.

"Yes, it was his idea," replied the priest. "He personally called me yesterday. And what's more, he wants you to be the assistant to his personal secretary until the time of your ordination to the priesthood. That is, if this is all acceptable to you?"

"Of course it is," answered Peter, with an obvious look of excitement. "What a wonderful opportunity to see and understand the inner-workings of the Church," he thought to himself.

"Excellent," replied Father Gaudini. "The date for your ordination to the diaconate will be a week from Saturday."

In a few short days Peter was transformed into the ranks of the ordained as he became a transitional deacon. And a deep transition did indeed progress within him.

Having a room right next to Cardinal Kullinzer and spending nearly all his waking hours with him and his secretary, Monsignor Hoppe, were not only opening Peter's eyes to the complex inner-workings of the Church, but also brought him into the influence of two more holy men of prayer.

Peter was deeply impressed by how everything that the Cardinal did was encircled with prayer. A deep awareness of Christ's presence radiated from him at all times.

Peter had the opportunity to meet the leaders of all the Vatican Congregations and many of their staff, although, of the meetings he accompanied the Cardinal on, the most memorial, by far, were those with the Pope.

Usually the Cardinal would meet with the Holy Father every day, and sometimes they would even meet more than once a day, but always the Pope's intricate understanding of situations, uncanny wisdom, and great compassion for people would hold Peter spellbound while in his presence.

Peter would never forget the first time that the Pope had spoken directly to him. The Holy Father spoke in English, but Peter's tongue got all tied up in his mouth, and he could hardly reply.

From that time on though, the Pope would speak to Peter in a different language each time they would meet, making a sort of game of seeing if he could find a language that the young deacon could not understand. When Peter would answer in the Holy Father's chosen language, the Pope would often laugh right out loud and say, "You have indeed learned your lessons well, Deacon Peter."

The Holy Father displayed a personal interest in Peter. He asked him about his family and many different things, such as how he perceived what was happening with the Church in America.

Peter felt like he was in a wonderful whirlwind. Never would he have considered it a remote possibility for himself to be speaking with the Pope in such personal ways. These were most definitely marvelous days.

Although, Peter knew those times, such as he was experiencing at the Vatican, would not last forever. Soon he would be a priest; he would be leaving all that he loved in Rome for a new experience. And once again he would be surprised with the direction God would give his life.

After one of the Cardinal's meetings with the Pope, the Holy Father asked Peter, "Deacon Peter, I understand you are now ready to become a priest?"

"Yes, Holy Father, I believe that I am, although I still am learning new and exciting things each day," answered Peter, not wanting to seem unsure of his calling, which he definitely was not, and yet, not wanting to sound proud in any way.

"Well, if your mastery of Theology, Sacred Scripture, and Cannon Law are anything like your mastery of the languages, I am also very sure of your readiness," replied the Pope with a broad smile on his face. "And from what I have been told, your preparation is more than adequate.

"Always remember, though, my son, that it is the Lord's work which we do; it is His strength that we must have in order to accomplish His work in the world. Knowledge and understanding are indeed very helpful, but above all things a priest must be a man of deep faith. I believe you are that type of man, Deacon Peter, and, if you will allow, I would appreciate the honor of presiding at your ordination."

"Yes! I would like that very much, Your Holiness," replied Peter, most pleasantly surprised.

"Then it shall be done," pronounced the Pope.

And so, it was in a few short weeks that Peter found himself, along with two of his fellow English-speaking seminarians, awaiting entrance into the sanctuary of Saint Peter's Basilica, for ordination into the priesthood.

Peter's brothers and sisters were there with their families. It was a wonderful reunion for them all. Over the past three days, Peter had been showing them some of the most interesting points of Rome, especially the Vatican. All of them had been greatly captivated by the Christian heritage proclaimed within Vatican City. Most of all, they would never forget the short visit with the Holy Father that Peter had arranged.

As Peter looked out from within the sacristy, he could see many familiar faces gathering in the sanctuary of Saint Peter's. Assembled there were the fellow seminarians who filled up several pews on the left side of the altar, the instructors who had taught him, many people who worked at the Vatican whom he had come to know, and his family.

Waiting with Peter in the sacristy were the other two men to be ordained; two seminarians, who would serve as altar-servers; Father Gaudini, rector of the Angelicum, who would be the master-of-ceremony; and a special visitor, who would assist Father Gaudini—Father Crowley had come over from England for Peter's ordination. Peter was deeply moved by Father Crowley's unexpected presence.

There was one person whose presence Peter would miss. Father Marks would not be able to attend. Whatever sense of loss Father Marks' absence brought was more than covered by the overwhelming joy that Peter felt for him at that moment. Peter knew that in a few days he would be leaving Rome and seeing Father Marks. Not only that, but he now knew that soon he would be working very closely with Father Marks. Although he would have to get used to his new title.

With the breaking apart of the Church in America, Bishop Bill was, of course, one of those who helped form the American Catholic Church, leaving the Roman Catholic Church with no bishop in the Glory Falls Diocese. The good news was that the Holy Father had named a man of rock-solid faith and integrity as the new bishop—Bishop Marks. But, there was much work to do in the diocese. Nearly half the priests had left with Bishop Bill. Surprisingly, when it came right down to leaving the

Church, even though there had seemed to be more dissenters in the Church, only about ten-percent of the lay people had left to join the new church. Reassuring, too, was the fact that every day brought a priest or two, who found the new church not as fulfilling as they had expected, back to the Roman Catholic Church.

There was one other bit of joyful news that Peter had heard: Bishop Marks had called Father Strong out of retirement to pastor Saint Alphonsus Parish. Father Strong, the priest who had baptized Peter as an infant, had been driven into retirement way before his time because he refused to bow down to pressure to deviate from the true teachings of the faith. Though he was now in his early eighties, he was in excellent health, and had kept active mentally and spiritually by personally ministering around the country at a pace that would have worn out many men half his age.

Peter's thoughts also turned to his mother and father and how he hoped that they would be pleased with the direction of his life. He prayed that, though he could not see them, they would be here with him one on his right side and one on his left.

He prayed also that God would strengthen and guide him this day and every day, making him worthy for the calling that He had given him. He thanked God for revealing His ways to him, especially through the ministry of His angel, Revealael. Peter wondered how many ways Revealael had helped him over the years that he had no knowledge of. And he wondered where he would be today if Revealael had not visited him.

Soon Peter's thoughts were interrupted by the arrival of the Holy Father and Cardinal Kullinzer, whom had both been so kind to Peter over these past six months. He was sure that his small role in the inner workings at the Vatican would have a positive impact upon him for the rest of his life. It most surely gave him an appreciation for the universal scope of the Church.

Suddenly, the magnificent pipe organ filled the church with its sweet-flowing music and Peter found himself proceeding with the Holy Father, Cardinal Kullinzer, Father Crowley, Father Gaudini, the altar servers, and fellow deacons into the sanctuary.

Although hundreds of people were there, it seemed to Peter as though he was, in this special hour, alone with the Almighty. To him, Divine Providence had made this moment possible, and now would the Divine Presence be made manifest.

As they genuflected before the presence of the Lord, Peter felt God's loving presence intensely. When the Holy Father began to pray, it seemed to Peter as though his whole life existed for the holy act about to transpire and he was totally enraptured by the moment.

The Pope spoke in English to the three transitional deacons, and he asked the congregation to affirm their calling. The Holy Father went on to inform them of the role of teacher, priest, and pastor which they were seeking—roles which were hardly new to the three, who had worked hard to perfect their performance of them over the past several years.

When each candidate was asked to affirm his willingness to celebrate Christ's mysteries for the glory of God and the sanctification of His people, determination filled Peter's soul as he committed himself. His heart raced with joy in anticipation of serving the people of God.

Then, the three men promised obedience to the Bishop of Rome and to his successors. Peter did so unhesitatingly.

He was glad that he was receiving ordination from the Holy Father. How hard it could be in some places of the world, he thought, to pledge obedience to a local bishop. The ordeal in America had pointedly shown where the heart of some bishops had been.

Peter and the other two candidates then prostrated themselves upon the floor directly before the Pope, who was accompanied to his right side by the Cardinal. The Holy Father prayed the Litany of the Saints and then invoked the Holy Spirit upon the three. Peter was deeply moved as he felt the rush of the Spirit upon him, and he wanted to praise the Lord with all of his being.

In the short time of silence that immediately followed, Peter's heart cried out praise to the Almighty Lord, and he lifted his head ever so slightly so that he could gaze upon the tabernacle. It was then that he noticed the hem of a long, white garment belonging to someone standing on the step directly behind the Holy Father and the Cardinal.

"Who could that possibly be standing there," he thought.

Not wanting to raise his head conspicuously high, but yet, still, curious as to who was there, he strained to his left to see the feet of Father Crowley and Father Gaudini, then to the right to see the two altar servers. Everyone was were they should be.

Somehow an additional person had joined them. It didn't seem possible, but it was true. Whoever it was, they were standing in what must have seemed a very strange location to those gathered in the church.

Peter had to know who it was; he must. He raised his head slightly so that he might see the identity of the unknown person. Standing behind Pope and Cardinal was a tall figure with his hands raised high in prayer.

Orders

Filled with surprise, then joy, and finally humble understanding that brought wonder, Peter recognized the intruder to his ordination as someone he alone, no doubt, could see.

Words that they had last shared and the great impact they would have on the rest of his life echoed through his mind.

Standing there, towering over Pope and Cardinal, was Revealael!

AURORA ANGELS

Epilogue

Now, therefore is given
the words and the visions
that have been received.
And understand that this
you must know:
Although mysteries often remain mysteries,
this mystery has been revealed to you:
"The time is short and the end is near,
but Armageddon, no one knew!"

To order additional copies of

AURORA ANGELS
Messengers to the Age of Armageddon

send $12.99 (Michigan residents add 6% sales tax) plus $3.95 shipping and handling to:

Praise Publishing
15955 15 Mile Road
Big Rapids, MI 49307

or have your VISA or MasterCard ready and call:

1-231-796-4995

Scriptural prayer books by L.E. London

The Seven-Day Scriptural Rosary
Two favorite devotions–Scripture reading and the Rosary–combined in one inspiring devotional.
0-87973-524-4, paper, 128 pages, $5.95
0-87973-192-3, two 90-minute audiocassettes, $14.95

The Passion Novena
A set of nine Scriptural Rosary mysteries allows you to reflect on the passion of the Lord. Perfect for Lent.
0-87973-733-6, paper, 136 pages, $5.95
0-87973-186-9, five audiocassettes, $24.95

The Salvation Novena
A set of nine Scriptural Rosary mysteries centered on the story of salvation. This devotional is ideal in helping one prepare for Advent and Christmas.
0-87973-917-7, paper, 136 pages, $6.95
0-87973-918-5, five audiocassettes, $24.95

To order send amount (MI residents add 6% sales tax) plus $3.95 shipping and handling to:

Praise Publishing
15955 15 Mile Road
Big Rapids, MI 49307

or have your VISA or MasterCard ready and call:

1-231-796-4995

Other books by L.E. London

Shadow of the Shroud
THE STORY OF CHRIST'S BURIAL CLOTH

The Shroud of Turin
What is the Shroud?
Where has it been over the years?
Why has its early history been hidden?
Who made the man's image on this famous cloth?
How could a negative image be faked 650 years ago?
Why can't science discover how it was made?
What is the story of the Shroud?

Follow the Shroud as it travels the Mediterranean world in a 2,000 year journey of faith, hope and love...

Discover historical fact and fiction woven together into an edifying story of the Lord at work in the shadow of **Christianity's Greatest Relic**.

The Shroud has changed a multitude of lives. It could change *yours*!

"**Shadow of the Shroud**: *The Story of Christ's Burial Cloth* is entertaining, thought-provoking, highly recommended Christian novel."
—***The Midwest Book Review***

---

from **Praise Publishing**
ISBN 0-9674425-5-9, 224 pages, paper, $11.99

REVELATION UNSEALED
A PROPHETIC MESSAGE FOR OUR AGE

by L.E. London

Finally, from the first verse to the last, a complete explanation of the Book of Revelation for the average Christian. In this dawn of the new millennium, when so many bold claims surrounding the end-times abound, this book is a faithful guide for understanding the powerful message that the Lord Jesus entrusted to his followers.

With Scripture, verse-by-verse commentary, study outline, symbolism key, map and topic reference, this book is suited for group Bible studies as well as for individual study and reference.

Revelation's prophetic message was intended to console and guide the Church. It was given so that it could be understood by every Christian. If one looks diligently to the Bible, it is still understandable today!

"This is a very sane commentary on the Book of Revelation and would be a helpful resource for adult Bible-study groups, especially those devoting their attention to this sometimes confusing and always fascinating book of Sacred Scripture." —*The Catholic Answer*

ISBN 0-9674425-4-0, 288 pages, paper, $12.99

To order any book from Praise Publishing:
send amount (Michigan residents add 6% sales tax) plus
$3.95 shipping and handling to:

**Praise Publishing
15955 15 Mile Road
Big Rapids, MI 49307**

or have your VISA or MasterCard ready and call:

1-231-796-4995